Sophie's Friendship Fiasco

Other books in the growing Faithgirlz!™ library

The Faithgirlz!™ Bible

NIV Faithgirlz!™ Backpack Bible

My Faithgirlz!™ Journal

The Sophie Series

Sophie's World (Book One)

Sophie's Secret (Book Two)

Sophie Under Pressure (Book Three)

Sophie Steps Up (Book Four)

Sophie's First Dance (Book Five)

Sophie's Stormy Summer (Book Six)

Sophie and the New Girl (Book Eight)

Sophie Flakes Out (Book Nine)

Sophie Loves Jimmy (Book Ten)

Sophie's Drama (Book Eleven)

Sophie Gets Real (Book Twelve)

Nonfiction

Body Talk

Beauty Lab

Everybody Tells Me to Be Myself but I Don't Know Who I Am

Girl Politics

Check out www.faithgirlz.com

faithGirLz! the beauty of believing

SOPHIE'S Friendship Fiasco

Nancy Rue

ZONDERVAN.com/
AUTHORTRACKER
follow your favorite authors

We want to hear from you. Please send your comments about this book to us in care of zreview@zondervan.com. Thank you.

ZONDERKIDZ

Sophie's Friendship Fiasco
Previously titled *Sophie Breaks the Code*

Requests for information should be addressed to:

Zondervan, *Grand Rapids, Michigan 49530*

Library of Congress Cataloging-in-Publication Data

Rue, Nancy N.
[Sophie breaks the code]
Sophie's friendship fiasco / Nancy Rue.
p. cm. – (Sophie series ; bk. 7) (Faithgirlz!)
Summary: When Sophie's efforts to protect her friends from a group of mean-spirited popular girls lead to misunderstandings at home and at school, she turns to Jesus for help.
ISBN 978-0-310-71842-0 (softcover)
[1. Bullies–Fiction. 2. Conduct of life–Fiction. 3. Imagination–Fiction. 4. Middle schools–Fiction. 5. Schools–Fiction. 6. Christian life–Fiction. 7. Virginia–Fiction.] I. Title.
PZ7.R88515Skf 2009
[Fic]–dc22 2009003015

Published in association with the literary agency of Alive Communications, Inc., 7680 Goddard Street, Suite 200, Colorado Springs, CO 80920. www.alivecommunucations.com

Interior art direction and design: Sarah Molegraaf
Cover illustrator: Steve James
Interior design and composition: Carlos Estrada and Sherri L. Hoffman

Printed in the United States of America

---

09 10 11 12 13 14 15 16 • 24 23 22 21 20 19 18 17 16 15 14 13 12 11 10 9 8 7 6 5 4 3 2 1

So we fix our eyes not on what is seen,
but on what is unseen.
For what is seen is temporary,
but what is unseen is eternal.

—2 Corinthians 4:18

One

Sophie LaCroix groaned out loud in the hallway of Great Marsh Middle School. "Can I just say I loathe PE class?" she said.

"Is *loathe* a Fiona word?" Kitty said as she linked her arm through Sophie's. She giggled, the way she did at the end of almost every sentence.

"What's it mean?" said Maggie, who hardly ever giggled.

Fiona pushed aside the stubborn strip of golden-brown hair that was always falling over one eye and continued to lead the way down the hall toward the PE locker room. "It means 'hate,'" she said.

"Only it sounds smarter," said Darbie, who had an Irish accent. She gave a firm nod, making her own reddish bangs dance on her forehead.

"I don't feel very smart in this class," Sophie said. "Coach Yates is always yelling at me—and every time I try to explain something to her, my voice comes out all squeaky."

The Corn Flakes grinned at each other.

"Your voice always comes out all squeaky," Maggie said in her that's-a-fact way.

"That's just you, Soph," Fiona said. "You're just you, and we're all just us."

Sophie managed a little bit of a smile. Just being them was what made them the Corn Flakes. *Other* people might think they were ditzy and flaky and say the things they did were corny. But the Corn Flakes knew better.

"Hey, Cue Ball!" somebody yelled. Sophie felt her smile snap away.

"Get Kitty into the locker room!" Darbie said.

Willoughby and Fiona unlatched Kitty from Sophie, and Maggie shoved the three of them through the door with Darbie on their heels, just as Sophie felt her quilted hat being plucked off her head. She grabbed at her glasses so they wouldn't go too.

"Catch, Eddie!" Colton Messik cried.

Sophie saw Eddie Wornom's belly bulge out from under his shirt as he jumped up and caught Sophie's hat. *Ewww*, she thought. Eddie hurled it at Tod Ravelli, whose face came to its usual point as he slam-dunked the hat into the trash can.

"Score!" Colton's grin seemed to spread from one stuck-out ear to the other. "Hey, Cue Ball," he said to Sophie. "You're bald!"

Like you haven't told me that a bazillion times, Sophie thought.

She waited until the boys had shoved each other into their locker room before she went calmly to the trash can and fished out her hat.

At least they didn't get to Kitty, she told herself as she pushed it down over her shaved head. *That's all that matters*. After all, she couldn't expect Fruit Loops like them to understand how a Corn Flake could part with all her hair to keep a sick friend from being the only girl in the whole school who was bald.

When Sophie got to her locker, the other Corn Flakes were almost changed into their PE clothes. Willoughby slung her arm around Sophie's shoulder and pressed their cheeks together, her almost-dark curls tickling Sophie's face. She was the only one of them who was short enough to do that — and even she was a few inches taller than tiny Sophie. "You're the best," she said in her bouncy voice.

"Trash can again?" Fiona said.

Sophie rolled her eyes.

Maggie shook her head at Kitty, so hard that her Cuban-dark hair splashed against her cheeks. "Boys are just lame."

There was a grunt from a few lockers down. Julia Cummings, the tall leader of the Corn Pops, tossed back her auburn hair.

"Someday you'll grow up and change your mind," Julia said.

She smirked at Anne-Stuart, one of her fellow "popular" girls, who gave the usual juicy sniff. She was pale and thin, and Sophie had never known her not to need a Kleenex.

"Grow up?" said B.J., the chubby-cheeked Corn Pop. "I don't *think* so."

A girl who had strawberry-blonde hair trailing down her back laughed — *way* loud — and looked at Julia like a puppy waiting for a treat. She was Cassandra Combs, the newest Corn Pop wannabe.

Sophie hoped the Pops would leave, but they just went back to putting on lip gloss. Sophie went into slow motion as she turned to the locker she and Kitty shared, dialing each number on the lock with precise care.

"You're gonna be late one of these days," Maggie said.

Willoughby went into the arm motions for a cheer. "Class won't be so bad today, Soph. All we're doing is running the track, and if you keep going Coach Yates won't yell at you."

"Coach Hates," Fiona put in.

Sophie kept her eyes away from them. "It takes me longer because I'm helping Kitty," she said.

Kitty peeled off her bright pink T-shirt, revealing the tiny "porthole" in her chest just above her bra. Kitty had leukemia, and the hole was where a tiny tube had been inserted so the doctors could give her the chemotherapy medicine—which hopefully would stop her disease—through the tube instead of having to give her shots. Sophie crowded in close until Kitty pulled on the white tee with GMMS—for Great Marsh Middle School—sprawled across the front in the red and blue school colors.

"Thanks, Sophie," Kitty whispered as she slipped off the quilted hat that matched Sophie's. Sophie replaced it at lightning speed with a red bandanna.

Only when Kitty's bald head was covered did Sophie step back. So far most of the Corn Pops hadn't seen the hole or gotten a close-up view of Kitty's head, and Sophie wanted to keep it that way. Even though chemotherapy had made all Kitty's hair fall out, Sophie and the Corn Flakes thought Kitty's naked head made her blue eyes seem bigger and bluer than ever and her tiny nose look even more like a piece of fine china.

But Sophie knew there would be no end to the Corn Pops' blurting out things like, "I wouldn't even come to school if I looked like that!"

Just as she always did, Sophie whipped off her own cap like a knight removing his armored helmet at the end of a tournament, revealing her peach-fuzzed head before she tied on her bandanna.

Kitty giggled. "You're so brave, Sophie."

"They can't hurt me," Sophie said. "Besides, it's only hair."

"Or lack of," Fiona said. She stood up from tying her tennis shoes. "You coming?"

"I'm not ready yet," Sophie said. "I was helping Ki—"

"You were foostering about, is what you were doing," Darbie said.

Maggie gave a matter-of-fact nod. "You're gonna get detention if you aren't there when Coach Yates blows her whistle."

"Your father will take your camera," Fiona put in, "and then we won't be able to make our next movie— "

"I'm *coming*!" Sophie snapped. All five pairs of eyes widened, and Sophie softened her voice. "You guys go ahead, okay?"

The Flakes left. So did the Pops, finally. Sophie could now get into her gym clothes without them seeing that, unlike every other seventh-grade girl on earth, she didn't even wear a bra yet. She still looked exactly the way she had in sixth grade. It didn't take much to imagine what the Corn Pops would do if they saw that.

Sophie put her PE shirt between her teeth, letting it hang in front of her while she unbuttoned her top. She would just have time to wriggle out of the blouse, yank the shirt over her head, and tear outside to get in line before roll check started.

Just as she parted her teeth and let go of the T-shirt, Sophie heard sneakers squeal to a stop on the floor a few feet away. Cassandra was staring at Sophie's bare chest, mouth open so her pale blue braces gleamed.

"Oh, my gosh!" she said. "I thought you were a boy!"

Somehow Sophie got her shirt pulled on and ran past Cassandra and out to her line just as Coach Yates was ending the long toot on her whistle. The coach, her too-tight, graying ponytail pinching her face, gave Sophie a look with a warning in it. Sophie was just glad she didn't yell. They'd found out the first day that this lady could bellow like an elephant. What really stunk was that they had her for PE *and* sixth period Life Skills. That was a lot of bellowing.

Coach Yates blasted out the order for them to run twice around the track, and Cassandra gathered the Corn Pops around herself. They took two steps and exploded into high-pitched shrieks and turned around to gawk at Sophie's chest. She was sure they were going to rush up to her and rip off her T-shirt just to check out Cassandra's story.

"Now what are they up to?" Darbie said at Sophie's elbow.

"Something heinous, guaranteed," Fiona said.

Sophie moaned inside. Fiona's favorite word for evil, *heinous*, was perfect for this situation.

"I know exactly what they're doing," Willoughby said. "Don't forget I was a Corn Pop before you guys saved me from them." She nodded wisely. "Cassie's trying to pass one of their tests for being accepted into the Corn Pops. She has to tell them something they can use for ammunition."

Sophie's stomach went into an immediate knot.

"What do you think it is?" Kitty said.

"What was yours when you got into the Corn Pops, Willoughby?" Sophie said quickly. The Corn Flakes shared everything, but this situation was way too embarrassing, even in front of her best friends on the planet. Her heart started to knot up too.

"You don't even want to know," Willoughby said.

"Let's get a move on, ladies—or you'll be doing three laps!"

They all broke into a run at the sound of the coach's roar, except for Kitty, who only had to walk as far as she could. Sophie peeked back at her over her shoulder. Kitty looked so small and puffy-faced and quivery all by herself. She and the rest of the Flakes had tried hanging back with her before, but Coach Hates had said a big-time NO to that.

"No Corn Pop better say an evil word to Kitty," Fiona said.

"We can't do anything evil back to them if they do," Maggie said.

"Our blasted code," Darbie said. "Sometimes it's a bit of a bother."

The Code was actually the thing Sophie loved most about the Corn Flakes. They had vowed never to put anybody down, even though people did it to them. The also vowed not to fight back or give in to bullies, and instead take back their power to be themselves. And they promised to talk to Jesus and obey God's Word, because God gave them the power to be who they were made to be. The Code made Sophie feel noble, like a maiden from medieval times who was as honorable as any knight of the Round Table—

Her name was Aurora, and she was the leader of six young maidens. She had led them to the Code and they lived by it, vanquishing vixens and villains with sheer goodness.

Willoughby gave Sophie a poke that brought her out of her dream world. She was pointing at the Corn Pops, who were a half lap behind them. They all had their heads leaning toward Cassandra, who still appeared to be enchanting them with her tale.

There isn't THAT much to tell about one flat chest, Sophie thought.

"I think Cassie passed her first test," Willoughby said.

"So what's her next one?" Fiona said.

"Now she has to do something about whatever she just told them."

Sophie swallowed hard.

"They're gonna get in trouble if they do anything to *us*," Maggie said. Sweat was making plastered-down sideburns in front of her ears. "After all the stuff they got caught for at the end of last year."

Fiona turned around to run backward so she could face them. "That was a whole different school though. The teachers here don't know about all that. The Pops are starting over with a clean slate."

"No fair," Maggie said. "We have to keep them from making fun of Kitty."

Sophie put a hand on her knotty side. They could protect their Kitty, she knew. But she wasn't sure how she was going to protect *herself* now that Cassie had seen—

But then she shook her head. *It doesn't matter,* she thought. *I won't LET it matter. They can't hurt me.* She tried to ignore the knot that was now twisting the *rest* of her insides like a whole bag of pretzels.

I will hold up the Code like a Shield of Honor before me, Aurora vowed to herself. And I will turn my thoughts to another, more noble cause—which surely I will find, because I always do—

"This probably sounds lame next to having leukemia," Willoughby said, "but I'm scared about cheerleading tryouts."

Sophie pulled her mind back to the Flakes. "Why?" she said. "You're good."

"We should know," Fiona said. "We've been watching you practice twenty-four/seven."

"You're *so* gonna make it," Sophie said.

Willoughby shook her head. "You know the Pops will try to make me mess up."

"Yeah," Maggie said from several steps behind them. She was now puffing like a train. "They hate you worse than any of us right now because you dumped them."

Willoughby pushed a bunch of curls up from her neck. "If one of you would try out with me, I wouldn't be so scared of what they might do."

"Not me," Maggie said.

"You don't want me either," Darbie said. "With my long legs, I'll make a bags of the whole thing."

Fiona was already shaking her head. "I'd end up getting right in their faces if they even looked at you wrong."

"Sophie?" Willoughby said. "What about you?"

A laugh gurgled up out of Sophie's throat. "Are you kidding me?"

"I need *somebody*." Willoughby's voice quivered. "I can't do it by myself, and I want this really, really bad—"

Aurora drew in a breath, and with it came the courage she was so known for. I don't know the dance, she thought. But I must be at the side of my fellow maiden in her distress. Until she learns the power of the Code, I must stand by her—

Fiona snapped her fingers in Sophie's face. "Where did you go, Soph?"

"You have a new character, don't you?" Darbie said.

Without even hesitating, Sophie said, "Aurora—medieval maiden."

"Our next Corn Flakes production!" Fiona said.

Maggie grunted behind them. "Don't say anything else. We don't have the Treasure Book with us to write stuff down."

"But what about the cheerleading tryouts?" Willoughby said.

Sophie smiled what she hoped was an Aurora smile. "I'm there for you," she said.

Willoughby shrieked in that way that always made Sophie think of a poodle yipping. She tried to hug Sophie while they were running. They both got an extra half a lap from Coach Hates.

At the end of class, Kitty was all proud that she'd walked a quarter of the way around *one* lap. The Flakes carried her into the locker room, yelling, "Kitty rocks!"

Sophie ran in ahead of them to clear a space on the bench so they could set Kitty's wobbly self down. Something caught her eye as she rounded the corner. On Sophie's locker door were two wads of cotton stuck on with duct tape, and above them was a piece of paper with a message scrawled across it: *Use these under your shirt until you get some real ones!*

Behind her the Flakes were rounding the corner. Sophie's hand flew up to yank it off, but the tape wouldn't let go.

"What is *that*?" Darbie said.

Sophie got the cotton balls and the paper down just as the Corn Pops also came around the corner. When they saw Sophie, they smothered their mouths with their hands. Cassie sidled up to her and spit through her braces, "I'll show you where to put them."

The other three Pops collapsed in a heap as Sophie's Flakes looked on, baffled. Only Cassie's narrow face was Corn Pop cool.

"I know where to put them," Sophie said. She stuck the taped side of both cotton balls under her nose like a mustache and turned to the Flakes.

"You look like Albert Einstein!" Fiona said. The rest of the Flakes cackled.

Behind them, the Pops laughed even harder, but Sophie pretended they weren't there. She just helped Kitty out of her shirt without anybody seeing her porthole, keeping the cotton balls stuffed under her nose the whole time. Kitty giggled until her cap was safely back on her head.

But Fiona held Sophie back on the way to fourth-period math. Her bow of a mouth was pulled into a small pink knot. "Are they teasing you about not having a bra that's padded out to here like they have?" She held her hands six inches from her chest.

"You knew?" Sophie said.

"Hello! I'm your best friend! So who saw? Cassie?"

Sophie nodded.

"Figures," Fiona said. "She tries to make herself look like Jennifer Lopez or somebody."

Sophie laughed. "We're not supposed to say evil stuff about them."

"Even if it's true?"

"That's the Code," Sophie said.

Fiona sighed. "I know," she said. Then she gave Sophie a sideways grin. "But you have to admit: you got them with the mustache."

Sophie grinned back. Yeah, she definitely had.

Two

But as soon as Fiona and Sophie went into Miss Imes' math room, all mirth—as Fiona called it—disappeared. Sophie dreaded this class almost as much as she did PE.

She had barely dropped into her seat when Miss Imes said, "Sophie."

She was standing over Sophie's desk. With her dark eyebrows shooting like arrows toward her short, almost-white hair, Miss Imes pointed to her head and mouthed, *Off.*

This was the only class where the teacher made Sophie stick to the no-hats-in-class school rule. Kitty was allowed to keep hers on in the fourth-period section because she had a medical reason. Miss Imes had told Sophie the first day that she didn't qualify for that. Slowly Sophie slid her cap off and put it in her lap.

"Hey, Cue Ball," Colton Messik whispered.

Sophie ignored him and adjusted her glasses as she stared, unseeing, at the board.

"If it weren't for your face, I wouldn't be able to tell the front of your head from the back."

I can't WAIT to tell Fiona how hilarious he is, Sophie thought, rolling her eyes.

"Yeah, it's pretty weird back here," Colton whispered on. "It's like your nose is missing. And your eyes. Dude, somebody stole your face!"

I wish somebody would steal YOURS, Sophie thought. This would be so much easier if Kitty were in their class, instead of her and Maggie and Willoughby being in another seventh-grade section for academics. Sophie always felt braver when she was showing Kitty how to handle these ignorant little children.

Aurora slid her Sword of Vengeance back into its sheath and lowered her head. "Father," she whispered to God, "please forgive me for my evil thoughts." Aurora knew that revenge belonged to God alone. Her job was to protect her maidens by teaching them to live by the Code. A Code that came from the Father himself. With her eyes closed and her face turned up to the Light, she could feel his strength coming into her again—

"Sophie LaCroix."

Sophie opened her eyes. Miss Imes was scowling down at her.

"Class," she said. Her voice was brisk and pointy like her eyebrows. "Your first test is this Friday, and I warn you, if you are not prepared, you will most definitely fail it. You came to me highly recommended, and I expect top work. So far, with the exception of Tod and Fiona, very few of you are giving me that. Am I clear?"

Sophie nodded. After all, Miss Imes might as well have just *said* she was talking right to her.

I would LOVE to give you top work, Sophie thought as she hunkered down over her paper. *But I've hardly understood a thing you've ever put up on the board. I'm lost!*

Lost in a sea of numbers that even she, Aurora, could not navigate—

Sophie felt something tickle the back of her head. She forced herself not to turn around.

No wonder I'm having trouble concentrating in here, she thought. *I wish I could sit next to Fiona. She'd help me focus.*

But Miss Imes had scoffed at that suggestion when they'd made it the first day. "I don't think much math would get done," she'd said. "And besides, Fiona is going to be working ahead of the class. She has an excellent mind for mathematics."

Sophie felt the tickle on the back of her head again, but she simply wrote down the next problem and stared at it. For at least three minutes. She could hear Fiona coughing, the way she always did when she saw that Sophie might be drifting off into dream world. But it wasn't that this time. Sophie just didn't get it.

And heaven knew what Colton was still brushing against her head. The thought of him touching her made her feel like things were crawling under her skin.

Oh, gross—he isn't BLOWING on me, is he? Sophie thought with horror.

She couldn't stop herself this time. She slid her hand across the back of her head and flicked it a few times, like she was shooing a fly. The room erupted.

Miss Imes glared over the top of her half-glasses. The classroom went as still as a morgue. When she looked down again, Sophie started to pick up her pencil. But there was something black on the palm of her hand. It was smeared with something. Like ink.

She whirled around in time to see Colton passing a black Sharpie over his shoulder to Anne-Stuart, who smothered a thick laugh. Colton had been writing on the back of her head with a *Sharpie*? What was now permanently engraved on her scalp for every hyena in middle school to go into hysterics over?

Sophie wasn't sure what she would have done if the bell hadn't rung at that exact moment. She clapped her hat onto her head and mowed down three people trying to get to the door. Miss Imes met her there.

"Your citizenship grade is falling, Sophie," she said. "You'd better get serious."

When Sophie got out into the hall, Fiona was leaning against the outside railing next to Darbie, holding a piece of paper with a smiley face on it.

"I can't smile!" Sophie said.

"No, *eejit*," Darbie said, pronouncing "idiot" in her Irish way. "That's what Colton drew on the back of your noggin!"

"Can you get it off?" Sophie said.

They scurried for the restroom, the minutes before the next bell ticking away. Fiona scrubbed Sophie's head with soap and a paper towel, until Darbie announced that it wasn't budging.

"We'll all be getting detention if we don't get to lunch," she said.

Sophie punched her cap back on and they ran for the cafeteria. Maggie, Willoughby, and Kitty were waiting, and before Sophie could even sit down, Darbie said, "The Loops are being eejits again." She pulled up the back of Sophie's hat just enough for the Flakes to take a peek.

Flake eyes bulged and hands came up to mouths. But all Sophie saw was Kitty, staring in horror.

"You don't think he'll try to do that to ME, do you?" she said.

"No way," Maggie said. "We'll protect you."

Sophie squeezed out a giggle that she hoped was convincing. "Colton is *so* not an artist," she said. "Is this lame or what?"

A slow smile broke across Darbie's face. "He made a bags of it, that's for sure."

Fiona nudged Kitty. "You draw way better than him."

Sophie felt an idea pop up like a spring. "Can you make it look better, Kitty?" she said. "Anybody have any Sharpies?"

"I do." Maggie dug into her backpack. "What colors do you want?"

Sandwiches were left uneaten as Kitty went to work on the back of Sophie's head, amid much coaching from the other Flakes.

"Bigger lips!" Willoughby said.

"More eyelashes, Kitty," Fiona told her. "And draw in glasses too."

When Kitty was finished, they declared it was good enough for a TV cartoon.

"I wish I could do it on myself!" Kitty said. She giggled.

Darbie drew her eyebrows together. "I just wish we could drop the Code for once and do something back to those blackguards," she said.

Darbie pronounced it "blaggards," which Sophie loved, but she shook her head.

"No way," Sophie said. "Then we're as heinous as they are. I'm never breaking the Code no matter what happens. Besides—" She shrugged. "This is all small stuff."

"You're so good, Sophie," Darbie said.

Sophie trailed Fiona and Darbie on the way to science, her mind spinning. It was cool that Darbie thought she was good. Still, she was really glad they were going to their girls' group Bible study after school. She needed a good boost.

Mr. Stires, their science teacher, was at the door, cheerfully greeting them with his shiny bald head and his toothbrush mustache. As soon as Sophie was past him, she felt something tug at her backpack, and suddenly all her books were pouring out of it onto the floor. She leaned over to pick them up, and her hat fell too.

"Dude!" said Colton Messik from behind her. She felt him poke at the back of her head. "I didn't do *that* face!"

"Lemme see." Tod stepped on Sophie's science book to get behind her.

Sophie turned her head to give Tod a full view and then looked back at him. Everything came to a point at his nose, until he started to laugh.

"No, man," he said to Colton, "you can't draw that good. That is cool!"

"Shut up!" Colton said. He punched Tod in the side with his fist. "It's not funny!"

"Yeah, it is. Hey, Julia, check it out!"

Anne-Stuart arrived behind Sophie with Julia, and Sophie ducked her head forward so she wouldn't get nose gunk all over her when Anne-Stuart snuffled.

"That's cuter than your real face," Julia said to Sophie with an actual giggle.

"I know," Sophie said. "I'm thinking of having it done the same way." She grinned. "But I'm not going to let Colton do it."

By now the entire class was crowded around Sophie's head. Right in front were Darbie and Fiona, who were giving her thumbs-ups and jerking their heads toward the Loops and Pops. Sophie had to agree that their usual enemies were looking impressed.

Except for Colton, who gave Tod a shove. "It's lame, man—it's stupid."

Tod, Julia, and Anne-Stuart stared at him, and Sophie watched the realization spring into their eyes one by one: they had forgotten they were supposed to think everything Sophie and her friends did was dumb.

"That is, like, such an immature thing to do," Julia said, tossing her mane.

"But it's so Sophie," Anne-Stuart said.

Tod pointed his finger at Sophie and gave a hard laugh. "Lame again," he said.

Aurora pushed away the inner knot that strained against her brocade gown. I have nobler causes, she reminded herself. I must protect the sickly Katrina, and the happy Willow, who so much wants to dance. The words of vixens and villains cannot hurt me.

Sophie felt a smile, the kind Fiona always described as wispy, spread across her face. *The Code of the Medieval Maidens* was going to be such a great film.

The minute the Corn Flakes got to the Bible study room at church after school, Fiona made Sophie take off her hat so Dr. Peter could see her decorated scalp. His eyes twinkled behind his glasses, which he pushed up by wrinkling his nose.

"That's a hoot!" he said. He ran his hand over the back of his head. "The barber cut mine so short this time, I could have one of those done too."

"You can't do it," Maggie said, her voice Maggie-factual. "You're a grown-up."

He grinned at her. "Don't spread that around," he said.

He lowered himself into a beanbag chair like the ones all the girls were sitting in—Gill and her friend Harley, who were two of the very-cool athletic girls the Corn Flakes called Wheaties, plus Fiona, Maggie, Willoughby, Darbie, and Sophie. Kitty wasn't with them. She was too tired at the end of the school day to do anything except take a nap.

But Kitty's pink beanbag was there beside Sophie's purple one, as empty as the Kitty-place inside Sophie. She always tried to make sure Kitty got to Bible study. When she had first found out she had leukemia, Kitty had been afraid she would die and not go to heaven. Sophie and Dr. Peter had been helping her get to know Jesus so she wouldn't be afraid of that anymore. Dr. Peter even went to Kitty's house and taught her the lessons when she couldn't be in class. Still, Sophie wanted her there, right beside her, so she could be sure Kitty was getting it—

"All right, ladies," Dr. Peter said. "Open up your Bibles to Luke 22:31–34."

Sophie picked up the Bible with the purple cover. All their Bible covers matched their beanbags—that's how amazing Dr. Peter was. She was totally ready to put herself right into the story they were about to read, which was the way Dr. Peter taught them. With any luck, it would help her with the Corn Pop/Fruit Loop situation, not to mention Miss Imes and Coach Yates—

"Now," Dr. Peter said, "we're at the end of Jesus' time with his disciples, and they're having their last supper together. Let's try to imagine—"

Sophie didn't even have to hear the rest of the instructions. Dr. Peter had been her special therapist for all of sixth grade, and he had taught her how to put herself in the Bible stories to help with all the heinous things she'd had to deal with back then. Now that he was their Bible-study teacher, she got to work on it even more.

Sophie closed her eyes and decided to be Simon Peter himself. It wasn't even that hard to pretend she was a boy anymore.

Something poked at Sophie's insides. "*I thought you were a boy!*" Cassie New Pop had said. "*Use these until you get some real ones.*"

"Everybody ready?" Dr. Peter said.

Sophie replaced the Cassie thoughts with an image of herself, sitting on the floor near Jesus.

Jesus is so easy to listen to, Sophie/Simon thought. *Not only is everything he says like warm bread in my mouth, but his eyes—his eyes are always so kind, even when they're stern. Sophie/Simon could never get enough of the way Jesus looked at her—as if no matter how much she messed up, he would help her be better—*

"Jesus has told them that one of them is going to turn him over to the people who want to kill him," Dr. Peter said. His voice sounded far away. "And that has shaken everybody up pretty good."

"*I would never do that!*" Sophie/Simon shouted to herself.

"And now Jesus is going to tell Simon Peter that Satan will test the disciples, especially him."

Dr. Peter began to read. Sophie kept her eyes shut tight and her mind wrapped around Simon Peter, his bread still in his hand as he listened—

" 'Simon, Simon,' " Dr. Peter read, " 'Satan has asked to sift you as wheat. But I have prayed for you, Simon, that your faith may not fail. And when you have turned back, strengthen your brothers.' "

Sophie/Simon felt her neck go stiff, and she dropped the bread onto the plate.

" 'Lord, I am ready to go with you to prison and to death,' " Dr. Peter read.

Sophie/Simon's heart was beating hard as Jesus turned to her.

" 'I tell you, Peter, before the rooster crows today, you will deny three times that you know me.' "

Sophie/Simon shook her head, over and over, even as Jesus looked into her with his kind eyes.

"You're kidding, right?" Fiona said.

Gill raised her hand. "There's no way he said he didn't know Jesus. Couldn't happen."

"You're going to find out in your homework reading," Dr. Peter said. "But let's talk about this some. Do any of you think you would deny you knew Jesus?"

"How about NO!" Sophie said. The rest of the girls shook their heads.

Dr. Peter sat forward in his beanbag. "You're right. You don't deny him — but all of us mess up on letting him be as important in our lives as we should."

"Mess up how?" Fiona said.

"Sometimes we get too busy to pray," Dr. Peter said.

Sophie knew she was okay there. Every night she imagined Jesus, the way Dr. Peter had taught her to, and talked to him. Sometimes she even did it during the day.

"Not reading the Bible is another one."

"We're good on that one," Willoughby said. "We're here!" Sophie thought she was going to break into a cheer.

"Okay, here's another one. When we worry and try to fix everything on our own, we're denying that God can help us and that he wants to help us."

There were head shakes and head bobs. Sophie scratched under her nose. *I really don't worry that much*, she thought. *God gave us our Code and we follow it, so we're really okay — except in PE — and math —*

There was a thinking silence.

"Just think about it and watch for it," Dr. Peter said. His eyes twinkled. "Nobody has to confess right now."

Fiona grinned at him. "That's good, because I could be here for days!"

Amid the laughter, Aurora stroked her Shield of Truth. Was it really so amusing, she wondered, to think of one's denials of the

Code? She sighed from the depths of her golden soul. There was much to teach the maidens. But leading them into Truth would be the noblest thing she had ever done. Even though she didn't know where to start, she knew God would show her how. Hadn't she already been guided to dance beside the maiden Willow so she wouldn't have to dance alone? Hadn't she already stood up to the villains and vixens for the maiden Katrina, all with the Spirit of Mirth? What was there she could not do as long as she stayed with the Code—which she most certainly would?

"You going to sit here all day like Miss Muffet on her tuffet?"

Sophie blinked up at her own reflection in Dr. Peter's glasses. The room was empty, and the Flakes' voices were fading down the hall.

"Not Miss Muffet," Sophie said. "The medieval maiden Aurora."

Dr. Peter broke into a grin. "Are you working on a new film?"

"It's not just a film. I think it's going to teach the rest of the Flakes how important it is to stick to our Code—you know the one."

Dr. Peter nodded. In the last year, Sophie had told him all about everything Corn Flake.

"I can't wait to see how it turns out," Dr. Peter said. He squatted down beside her. "Just be sure you're giving Jesus equal imagination time. Especially if you feel like you're escaping into the maiden Aurora when you shouldn't be."

"I'm not," Sophie said. "I'm getting all my assignments done—well, except math, but I'm gonna try harder—and I'm getting along with Daddy and Lacie and everything."

He stood up, nodding, and Sophie scrambled out of the beanbag. "Just one more thing," he said. "Be sure you do the assignment for this class as soon as you can, okay? Because, Sophie-Lophie-Loodle, I think you just might be put to the test."

"Okay," Sophie said.

But on the way out of the room, she chewed on her lower lip. What assignment was he talking about?

Three

Sophie was going to ask Fiona about the Bible study homework during first period the next day when they got to their combined English/History class. But Ms. Hess, one of their two team teachers, was writing on the board in handwriting as bubbly as her voice:

Essay Assignment: YOUR Code of Honor

All other thoughts left Sophie's head. *I could write that essay in my sleep!* she thought.

As soon as the bell rang, Colton Messik stopped trying to nudge Sophie's tweed newsboy cap off with his pencil and said, "What's a Code of Honor?"

You wouldn't know one if it bit your head off, Sophie thought. For Pete's sake — they had only been studying the legends and the history of medieval times for three weeks. She had wondered more than once how Colton had ever gotten into this special honors block in the first place.

Ms. Hess' dimples appeared like two finger pokes in whipped cream. "Just to refresh your memory," she said, "King Arthur wrote one for his Knights of the Round Table so they would realize, for one thing, that might didn't make right. What else was in the Code, class?"

As usual, she was pronouncing her words very clearly, as if her lips were made of rubber. Their other team teacher, Mrs. Clayton, barely moved *her* mouth at *all* when she talked. It was as if the words were coming out of her long narrow nose with its horn-flare nostrils.

"Let's hear it," she trumpeted out.

Julia raised her hand. "Do what you ought to in spite of your fear?" she said. She cocked her head, letting one side of her thick tresses slide over a green eye. That, Sophie knew, wasn't for the teacher's benefit. It was for Tod Ravelli's. He and Julia were "going out"—although Sophie could never figure out exactly where they were "going." They were both twelve.

"Good job, Julia," Ms. Hess said.

Sophie looked quickly to see if she was talking about Julia's answer or her flirting techniques.

"What else?" Mrs. Clayton said. "Educate Colton."

No problem! Sophie thought. She shot her hand up. "Work for justice rather than power. Your word—"

"—is your most valuable possession!" Aurora cried out. She held up her shield. "Never take advantage of weakness but rescue the innocent—"

Sophie could hear somebody coughing, and she looked over at Fiona. She was hacking herself blue and pointing at Sophie's literature book—which she was holding in front of her in a shield-like fashion. She lowered it and hoped her face wasn't turning as red as it felt.

Mrs. Clayton gave Sophie a long look before she said, "Good," and turned to the class. "Now, in this essay we want you to describe the Code of Honor that you live by. We also want you to include the things that make it hard for you to stay true to those principles."

“What if I don’t have any principles?” Tod said without raising his hand. His brown spiky hair always stuck up farther than anything else on his short self anyway.

“You just make it up as you go along, huh, Tod?” Ms. Hess said.

The dimples appeared again. Between those, and the fact that Ms. Hess wore about a size 2 and had her ash-blonde hair flipping up from a crooked part, it was hard to tell her from the eighth graders.

“Works for me” Tod said. Then he leaned way across Darbie so he could high-five Colton.

“Tell us all about it in your paper,” Mrs. Clayton said to Tod. She didn’t bubble and dimple like Ms. Hess. She had blonde cemented hair and blue eyes like bullets. But she did twitch a smile at him. What, Sophie wondered, did teachers see in that kid?

“Let’s get started,” Mrs. Clayton said.

“How long can we make it?” Anne-Stuart said.

“Would you like it typed on the computer?” Julia said.

“Longhand is fine, and no more than two pages. You two are such perfectionists!” Ms. Hess shook her head at Mrs. Clayton, so that her zebra earrings wiggled back and forth.

There they go with the I’m-such-a-perfect-student routine again, Sophie thought.

She and the Corn Flakes had already figured out what that was about. Ms. Hess was the cheerleading adviser, so she would be one of the judges at the tryouts. The Pops weren’t going to take any chances of her finding out what they were *really* like.

Sophie looked at her paper and scratched under her nose with her gel pen. It was going to be easy to write what her Code of Honor was. But when it came to the things that got in the way of living the Code, it was going to mean telling how heinous the Corn Pops and Fruit Loops had been to them.

Wasn't that breaking the first rule of the Code: don't put other people down?

She closed her eyes and let Aurora come into view. She was bound to have some answers ...

Sophie's dad brought home dinner in two steaming boxes from Anna's Pizza that night.

"You kids are wearing your mother out," Daddy said. He deposited the boxes on the big square coffee table in the family room and nodded toward Mama, who was curled up on the couch. "She's too tired to cook."

Six-year-old Zeke let out a first-grader-style yelp and dove for the cheese and pepperoni. But Sophie and her older sister, Lacie, looked at each other with puzzled eyes.

Mama was too tired to cook? Sophie thought. *Mama cooks when she's been up all night with one of us that's barfing!*

"Okay, what's wrong?" Lacie said.

"She's taking the night off," Daddy said. He directed his dark blue eyes at Lacie. "Give your mother a piece."

"Uh, no," Mama said. She lifted one side of her upper lip. "Just some crust."

Oh, Sophie thought. *SHE's the one who was barfing all night.*

Come to think of it, Mama's face was pretty much as pale as her highlighted curls. And she didn't look so much wispy—the way people said she and Sophie both did—as she did puny. Yeah, that was the stomach flu all right.

Lacie and Zeke, on the other hand, both had dark hair and deep blue eyes like Daddy, and they were big-boned the way he was. Daddy had even started wearing his hair like Zeke's, stuck out in short, every-which-way spikes.

Daddy's the one that needs a hat, Sophie thought. While she reached for a piece of pizza, she automatically put her hand up to keep her cap from sliding off. It wasn't there.

She had forgotten to put it back on when she came downstairs. Oops. Mama and Daddy hadn't seen her other face yesterday. She'd kind of been hoping it would just wear off before they did.

"Hey—cooool!" Zeke poked a pizza-greasy finger at Sophie's scalp. "I want that on my head!"

"Do I want to know what he's talking about?" Daddy said.

Lacie turned Sophie around and let out a husky laugh. "No, you don't," she said.

Daddy took Sophie's head in his hands. She could feel his eyes boring into Kitty's drawing.

Please, God, make him think it's funny! Sophie thought.

"I think it's gonna make the Corn Pops and them stop teasing Kitty," Sophie said. "You know—we're showing them that they're not getting to us."

"That game plan could backfire," Daddy said. He was going into sports talk. Not a good sign.

He and Mama looked at each other and had a parent conversation without saying a word. Not a good sign either.

"What about your teachers?" Mama said. She was sitting up farther on the couch. *Definitely* not a good sign.

"None of my teachers have even noticed," Sophie said. "They all let me wear my hat except Miss Imes."

Lacie coughed.

"What?" Daddy said to her.

"Nothing. Choked on a pepperoni."

Daddy scratched his head. "We just don't want you creating a distraction in the classroom, Soph. We're all for you standing up for Kitty and making this easier for her, but you need to play your own zone too. You see what I'm saying?"

Sophie didn't, but she'd get Lacie to explain it later. She was athletic. She got the sports-talk thing.

"I'll make sure I'm not a distraction," Sophie said.

"You know you lose the video camera if you get into any trouble—" Daddy said.

"Ugh."

They all looked at Mama, who was closing the lids on the pizza boxes. "Would everybody mind taking their pizza to their rooms to eat? I just can't stand the smell right now."

Sophie was more than happy to grab a piece and escape to her bedroom and end *that* conversation.

Besides, she had to write her paper for Ms. Hess and Mrs. Clayton. If she was going to be such a loser in math, she had to make up for it in English, or her video camera was going to wind up in Daddy's closet.

As long as she didn't make worse than a B in any subject or get into trouble, she was allowed to use her video camera for Corn Flake Productions. If she messed that up, the camera was history for a while. She had never lost it yet in a whole year. Well, except for that one time ...

Sophie ate the pepperoni off the pizza and propped herself against a pile of pillows on her pink bedspread. With her notebook on her lap and the gauzy bed curtains cozying her into her own world, Sophie knew just how to get around putting down the Pops and Flakes in her paper. All other thoughts faded with the mist that hung over Camelot.

With her pen dipping in and out of the ink like a bird at a feeder, Aurora wrote lavishly of her beloved Code, the words streaming across the page, trying to keep up with her thoughts.

And then she grew troubled. Sir Peter had seemed to doubt her that day, talking about a test she would face. Didn't he realize that she had mastered all that he had taught her?

Aurora set down her pen and went to her window, winding herself up in the veil of curtains that muted the moonlight. He will see, she thought, that I—and all of my maidens—are ready to stand up to any test that is put before us.

"You are totally going to pull those down one of these days."

Sophie peeked out of the curtains to see Lacie sprawling across her bed. Sophie unwound herself, frowning.

"I'm doing my homework," she said as she joined Lacie among the pillows.

"I get it," Lacie said dryly. "Look. Let me give you some advice about Miss Imes."

"I heard you choking when I said her name," Sophie said. "Do you think she'll give me a detention if she sees my head?"

"Nah. Show me in the school handbook where it says that's against the rules. But— "

"I hate 'buts,'" Sophie said.

"If she sees it, she's going to think it's a distraction too. Just keep a low profile."

"How do I do that?"

"Do all your work. Don't pass notes or talk. Ace all your tests. Piece of cake."

Maybe for you, Sophie thought. Just as it was occurring to her that—du-uh—maybe Lacie could actually help her with math, Lacie said, "Same goes for Coach Yates."

"Coach Hates," Sophie said.

Lacie grinned as she went for the door. "You got it," she said.

Sophie smiled to herself when she finished her paper, with a pen-flourish, and turned out the light.

As soon as she took off her glasses and snuggled under the covers and closed her eyes, there was Jesus in her mind. She could just "see" him looking at her with his kind eyes, and she knew she could ask him anything she wanted to.

"Jesus?" she whispered. "Thanks for giving us the Code and for giving me so many friends who believe in it—and in you, of course. And could you just help me with whatever test Dr. Peter thinks I'm gonna get? Especially if it's a math test. They're the worst. And getting dressed for PE. I need help there."

She let out a long Sophie-to-Jesus sigh and waited. If she let her imagination give her an answer, it would be, *Sure, Sophie—next test, A—guaranteed. And when you wake up tomorrow, you'll have breasts like everybody else.*

But Dr. Peter had also taught her that she shouldn't put words into Jesus' mouth, because they would just be what she *wanted* him to say. Jesus always answered somehow if she just listened and paid attention. He was always nudging her forward to do something she didn't think she could manage alone. With Jesus there, she really wasn't doing it by herself.

She wriggled down farther under the covers. *As long as I follow the Code, I'm okay,* she thought sleepily. *And I always, always will.*

Four

The next day, when all the Code of Honor papers had been turned in, Mrs. Clayton told them to turn to page sixty-four in their literature books and read.

"This is the place in the legend," she blared out, "where he discovers that something vital to the success of his Round Table has completely been forgotten."

Sophie dug hungrily in her backpack for her book. There was bound to be more good stuff in the Arthur legend for the Corn Flakes to use in their film. *We need to get started*, she thought.

When Sophie sat back up, book in hand, her pen was on the floor, and Colton's foot was suspiciously close to it. Sophie held on to her pink-and-black-plaid hat with one hand and bent to retrieve the pen with the other. Colton gave it another nudge with his toe, pushing it out of reach. When Sophie let go of her hat so she could hold on to her desk with one hand and snatch up the pen with the other, *of course* Colton snatched her cap.

There were a few snickers close by. As Sophie turned around to get the hat back, she caught Fiona's look. There was a devilish gleam in her eyes as she held up her notebook, where she'd scrawled *Repeat yesterday*.

Sophie shifted her gaze to Colton, who was twirling her hat on his finger. Make a joke out of it? Was that what Fiona meant?

"You know what, Colton?" Sophie said out loud. "You really ought to get some new material." She grinned at him. "I'm over the knock-the-hat-off thing."

He watched her lips as she spoke, and Sophie noticed his ears sticking out on the sides of his head in that way Anne-Stuart always said was "SO cute!" *Ewww.* Sophie lifted the hat from his finger and perched it on her head.

"If you really want to wear it, you can," she said, "but I don't think it's your color."

The class roared, and Sophie turned back around, fixing her most innocent gaze on Mrs. Clayton, who was turning from the board to face them.

"All right," the teacher trumpeted out of her nose, "this is not Comedy Central. Get to work, people."

Ms. Hess was nodding. Even the pumpkin faces dangling from her earrings looked disapproving. When they turned to each other to exchange teacher glances, Colton hissed, "Real funny, Cue Ball. You're killin' me."

Sophie didn't answer. She was too busy watching Julia and Anne-Stuart give each other stunned glances. Sophie smiled smugly at Fiona.

When the bell rang at the end of their two-hour block, both Fiona and Darbie hurried over to Sophie, faces shining.

"That was *class*, Sophie!" Darbie said.

"Come on," Fiona said. She dragged Sophie toward the door. "I can't wait to tell Maggie and them."

"I wish we coulda been there!" Willoughby said when they were jogging around the track, minus Kitty. She gave one of her like-a-poodle laughs that sounded as if she had been there. The usual cartwheel came next.

"I have a question though," Maggie said. She had to talk between huffs. "Is it against the Corn Flake Code to make people laugh at those guys?"

"I don't see how," Fiona said. "We're not supposed to give them back what they give us, but since when were they ever as funny as we are?"

Darbie snorted. "If they tried, they'd make a bags of it for sure."

"We're not supposed to hurt people's feelings," Maggie said.

"Who says we're hurting their feelings?" Fiona said.

"They don't have feelings!" Willoughby said.

Darbie elbowed Sophie as they started the second lap. "Are you slagging them to hurt their feelings?"

"No," Sophie said. "Honest."

"Then why are you doing it?" Maggie said.

By now she had slowed to a walk and was several steps behind. They all slowed with her.

"I'm doing it," Sophie said, "so that maybe they'll see they aren't getting to us and they'll stop. It's to protect us." Sophie glanced over her shoulder at the lone figure three rows up on the bleachers whose back was curved like a lost puppy's.

"Oh," Darbie said. She looked at Kitty too. "It's decided then: funny comebacks—"

"They're called 'retorts,'" Fiona put in.

"—are not against the Corn Flake Code, as long as they don't hurt people and they're used only for our protection." Darbie ended with a definite nod.

"Yes!" Willoughby said.

They high-fived and broke into a run so they could get done and tell Kitty. Maybe at last, Sophie thought, this *was* a way to teach the Corn Pops. A way that was Code-worthy.

So, armed with Aurora's Spirit of Mirth, Sophie plunged fearlessly into territory she would have run cowering from before.

When chubby Fruit Loop Eddie Wornom lunged for Kitty's hat in the hall, Sophie told him he was three yards short of a touchdown. Sometimes it paid to have a sports freak for a father. Everyone laughed. Except Eddie.

When Colton pretended to throw up on their table in the cafeteria and left a rubber thing that looked like he really *had* upchucked, Sophie picked it up and said, "Uh, Colton? You left your lunch here. Did you make it yourself?"

And when Tod tried to imitate Darbie's accent during the lab experiment in fifth-period science class, Sophie asked him—oh so politely—if he had an impediment stuck in his throat. She loved it when he had to ask Julia what an "impediment" was. Julia didn't know either, which gave Fiona a chance to instruct them. Tod wasn't amused.

Once Sophie was on a roll, the rest of the Flakes joined in.

Darbie could be hilarious with her Irish slang, and Fiona's vocabulary seemed to strike most people as funny. Willoughby had a sense of the silly that cracked kids up, especially when she practically did a cartwheel after everything she said.

Kitty usually giggled so much she didn't have a chance to chime in. Maggie never did get the hang of it, so she just got the Corn Flakes Treasure Book that Fiona always kept and wrote everything down in there, in case they ever wanted to use any of it in a film.

But one of the best scenes happened without the Corn Flakes even planning it.

"I'm going to look like a moron at these tryouts today," Sophie said on Thursday during sixth period.

"I've seen you cheer, Soph," Fiona said. "I think you're right."

"So what are you going to do, Sophie?" Darbie said.

Sophie felt a slow grin easing onto her face. "The same thing we've *been* doing," she said.

So after school, with most of the seventh graders watching from the bleachers in the gym, Sophie cheered the cheer Willoughby had tried to teach her, only with her arms flapping and her legs tangling up. The goofy grin (Fiona said later) made Ronald McDonald look depressed. Sophie's final cartwheel and splits landed her upside down, glasses and toboggan hat sailing off, feet kicking in the air—but she was still yelling, "GO! FIGHT! WIN!" She got a standing ovation.

But even better than *that* was what Sophie hadn't expected. B.J. was called up next, and she was laughing so hard, she had to start over twice. Anne-Stuart's laughter put her into bronchial spasms, and she had to wait until last to go. Cassie kept it together until her final cartwheel, when she careened into the judges. The whole crowd howled because they thought she'd done it on purpose, just to outdo Sophie. It was obvious from the way Julia was twitching her pom-pom back and forth like a cat's tail that she was not pleased with any of them.

Only seven people made the squad. Cassie wasn't one of them. The rest of the Corn Pops made it, and so did Willoughby and three girls who had come to GMMS from different elementary schools. Willoughby told Sophie later that Ms. Hess said a few judges actually voted for Sophie, but that she had said she wasn't having Bozo the Clown on her squad.

Sophie didn't care about that because Kitty was still laughing—like she hadn't laughed in a long time.

Yes! Sophie thought. *I think I'm passing the test.*

"I actually think the Fruit Loops are starting to lay off us," Fiona said to Sophie before first period Friday morning. "We have them quaking in their Nikes."

In class, Ms. Hess told them to look up the definitions for next week's vocabulary words and write a sample sentence for each one.

"And you don't need to try to be funny," she said, American flags standing at attention on her earlobes.

"Aw, man!" Colton said.

But Sophie was sure from the way Ms. Hess moved her rubbery mouth in her direction that she was talking about her. Looking as studious as she could, Sophie wrote down the first word—*Virile: characteristic of an adult male; manly; masculine.*

I wonder what the female word is? Sophie thought.

Aurora looked at herself in the mirror, gazing at her finely toned muscles, studying the strength of her jaw. She was all woman, from her intelligent forehead to the chest that breathed only good. But as she slowly smiled at herself, she knew she would never wreak vengeance on the villains and vixens by making them quake. It would be purely through the Spirit of Mirth, the Shield of Truth, the Strength of the Code—

Aurora laughed her soft laugh. Her power was in being a maiden of the Code. The six maidens were strong. "But girls are girls," she said to the mist. "They are not merely soft boys—"

"I know that; thanks," said Colton behind her.

There was a hard chuckle from another corner. "You know it now that she *told* you!" Tod said.

"Shut UP!" Colton said.

"You would know that," Anne-Stuart whispered to Sophie, "Little Boy LaCroix."

"Enough!" Mrs. Clayton blared.

Sophie looked away and pretended to be intent on the next vocabulary word. Inside, she was stinging.

If they can't hurt me, she thought, *how come I feel like a swarm of bees just attacked me?*

She blinked at the word list. *Chivalry* came next.

A code of honorable behavior, she wrote.

Just like the Corn Flake Code.

Take back the power to be yourself.

Yes, she told herself. *Just laugh it off.*

At the end of the period Colton unzipped her backpack—again—so that everything fell out of it when she picked it up.

"I told you," she said to him as he walked backward out of the room, smirking at her, "you need some new material."

She waved the Flakes on and collected her books. It actually didn't bother her that much. If she timed it just right, she would be slipping into the locker room just as everybody else was leaving. She could still make it out to the line before Coach Hates blew that evil whistle. She wasn't sure she could laugh that off yet.

The only problem was that she wouldn't be there to help Kitty with her bandanna. One of the other Flakes could do it, but Sophie liked to make sure.

Okay, stop it, Sophie told herself as she double-timed it toward the locker room door. Which was really worse: her getting teased because she didn't need a bra, or Kitty getting a hard time because of her leukemia? *Well*, *duh*, Sophie thought.

She broke into a half-run, only to skid to a stop in front of the locker room. There was a computer-printed sign on the door that read:

> The boys' showers are not working.
> The locker rooms have been switched for today.
> All girls go to the boys' locker room.

That makes sense, Sophie thought as she headed for the other room. The girls hardly ever took showers in PE, but if the boys didn't—*Ewww*. Sophie pulled open the door of the boys' locker room and stepped inside. It was quiet, and it smelled like gross dirty socks and boy sweat, which burned a person's nose way more than girl sweat.

"Hello?" she said.

Her voice echoed back to her in its high-pitched-ness. Everybody must already be out on the field, and she was later than she thought.

Sophie hitched her backpack up some more and hurried around a tiled wall. Six feet from her, a boy was just pulling his shirt down over his hairy armpits.

Before she could turn and flee, a man even bigger than Daddy was blocking her, and from every side it seemed.

He had a shaved head and an eyebrow that went all the way across his forehead. His picture, she thought, must be next to the word *virile* in the dictionary. Only when Sophie spotted the whistle hanging from his neck did she realize he was one of the boys' coaches. She didn't know his name.

"Where do you think you're going?" he said.

Sophie nearly choked. His voice was almost as high-pitched as hers was. It didn't sound like it should be coming out of his barrel chest.

"You think it's funny, walking into the boys' locker room?" he said.

A giggle inched upward with every word he said. Sophie slapped her hand over her mouth.

Coach Virile narrowed his eyes into two pencil points. "What were you planning to do in here?"

Sophie sucked back the giggle. "Um, get dressed for PE," she said.

She tried to make her voice deeper, but she could see it didn't work. His eyes went from pencils to pins.

"If you're mocking me, you've got some hard time coming," he said.

"I'm not mocking you, honest!" Sophie said. "That's just the way I talk!"

Ewww. Even worse.

Sophie jerked her thumb toward the door. "The sign on the girls' locker room said we were changing in here today."

He *glowered*—a Fiona-word that was made for the way his one eyebrow hooded his eyes. He went out the door and down the few steps to the next door, with Sophie close behind. He ripped off the sign with two fingers.

"You actually thought this was for real?" he said in his soprano-like voice.

"I guess I did," Sophie said. "Silly me, huh?"

Sophie wanted to bite back the words as soon as they were out of her mouth. Coach Virile's sense of humor was obviously not as big as he was.

"Funny how nobody else took the bait," he said. "Who's your teacher?"

"Coach Hates—um—Yates!"

The eyebrow lowered. "You just don't know when to quit, do you? Get on to class—I'll be talking to Coach Yates."

I'm toast, Sophie thought as she dragged herself into the *right* locker room. The place was empty, and she knew that Coach Yates had long since called the roll by now. With visions of detention lurking in her mind, Sophie pulled open her locker. A piece of paper floated out:

> Little Boy LaCroix,
>
> In the future, please change in the Boys' Locker Room—where you BELONG!

I TRIED to change in there, she wanted to say to the Pops. *Thanks to you.*

Five

When Sophie got to the field, Coach Virile and Coach Yates were standing together. They bored their eyes into her at the same time.

"You got it handled?" Coach Virile said to Coach Yates.

Coach Yates nodded as Coach Virile jogged off to the boys' field, making the earth quake as he went.

"Somebody put a sign up, huh?" Coach Yates yelled.

Sophie knew putting her hands over her ears would *not* be a good idea. She nodded.

Coach Yates shifted her voice up to the next yell-level. "Admit it, LaCroix: you did it yourself. You're the little class clown—making a joke out of the cheerleading tryouts, getting the back of your head painted."

How does she know about all that? Sophie thought.

"I think you need a little attitude check." Coach Yates ran her eyes down her clipboard, face pinched by the ponytail as always. "Detention," she said. "After school—Wednesday. Be here."

She made a huge *T* next to Sophie's name. "It's not looking good for your citizenship grade," she said. "So I'd start adjusting before Wednesday. Four laps. Right now."

Sophie mumbled a "Sorry" and headed for the track. The other Flakes were finished running, and Sophie felt alone without them.

And I'm going to be even MORE alone when Daddy takes my camera and we can't make our medieval film—plus, I'll probably get grounded for LIFE.

But even that wasn't the worst.

When she got to math class, Miss Imes had written on the board: TODAY IS FRIDAY. YOU KNOW WHAT THAT MEANS.

"No!" Sophie said out loud. "Not the test!"

"Yes, the test!" Anne-Stuart said, in a voice that sounded like a stuffy-nosed version of Sophie's.

"Wait a minute though." Julia was cocking her head at Anne-Stuart. "Don't boys *like* math?"

Then they both turned to Sophie, barely hiding their smirks.

When Miss Imes passed out the tests and Sophie looked at hers, her heart took a dive for her knees. There wasn't a problem on there she knew how to do, and she'd totally forgotten to ask Lacie for help. There was only one thing to do.

Dear Miss Imes, Sophie wrote at the bottom of the test paper. *Something very strange has occurred, because I don't know how to do any of these problems. Maybe the math part of my brain got erased and it's been replaced by a more creative force. Or maybe I'm just dumb. I think I need help.*

When everybody passed their papers up, Sophie put hers on the bottom of the stack.

"All right, class," Miss Imes said, "I'm going to pass these out again, and we're going to grade them together. Please let me know if you get your own paper."

Dear Lord, Sophie thought, *PLEASE let Fiona or Darbie or one of the Wheaties get mine. PLEASE!*

But what if the Lord wouldn't give her a yes? After all, she realized with a lump in her throat, she hadn't imagined Jesus in two days. Every nerve was practically poking out of her pores as Sophie watched Miss Imes pass out the papers. When she got to the last one, she stopped, looked more closely at the sheet, and placed it facedown on Sophie's desk. "We'll talk after class," she said. The eyebrows were pointing.

While everyone else checked answers, Sophie tried not to give up hope of ever seeing her video camera again. Maybe Miss Imes hadn't read her whole note. Maybe when she saw that Sophie was asking for help, she wouldn't shoot her eyebrows into her scalp.

When the rest of the class left for lunch, with Fiona and Darbie mouthing questions at Sophie as they trailed out, Sophie tried to get Aurora in mind on her way to Miss Imes's desk, but the medieval maiden didn't show up.

"You're in trouble, aren't you, Sophie?" Miss Imes said.

No, Sophie thought, *I'm just math-retarded.*

"I know math is just not some people's thing," Miss Imes said. "But anyone can learn what I'm teaching in here."

Although Sophie wanted to say, *Anyone except me!*, she just nodded.

"But the further behind a student gets," Miss Imes went on, "the harder it is to catch up." She put on her half-glasses. "You haven't scored better than a D on a quiz in here yet, have you?"

"No, ma'am," Sophie said.

Miss Imes looked at Sophie over the tops of the half-glasses. "Do you WANT to pass the tests?"

"Yes, ma'am!" Sophie said. And then she completely lost her mind and said, "I'd like to drive right past every one of them!"

Miss Imes looked as surprised as Sophie felt. But she recovered first and said, "I keep the parents of my seventh graders very well informed of any difficulties their children are having—and your parents need to hear from me on a number of levels. Not the least of which is your attempt to amuse the entire class with that other face you're wearing."

Sophie couldn't swallow. It felt like there was a hippopotamus in her throat.

Miss Imes took off the glasses and folded them neatly. "But I am going to give you one more chance to prove to me that your failure is not simply because you fool around too much. I am going to assign you an in-class tutor."

Sophie gulped over the hippo. "I'll prove it," she said. "Fiona knows how to help me."

"What makes you think it's going to be Fiona?" Miss Imes said. She nodded toward the door. "You'd better go to lunch."

No, Sophie thought as she dragged herself to the cafeteria, *I'd better go to a dungeon and have them lock me up there so Daddy can't find me.*

When Sophie got to the Flakes' table, Maggie had the purple Treasure Book open.

"We need to get started on our film," Fiona said. "Before we go nuts."

Sophie sagged into a seat. "There might not *be* another film," she said.

"Miss Imes," Maggie said.

Sophie nodded miserably. "I'm failing in there, and she's gonna call my parents unless I pass the next quiz. She's giving me a tutor. Only she said it might not be Fiona."

Kitty slipped her hand into Sophie's and gave it a weak squeeze.

"Who's she gonna give you then?" Willoughby said. "Fiona's the smartest person in this whole school in math."

"She's gonna give me to you, Soph," Fiona said. Her little bow mouth was firm. "She's just trying to scare you."

"Work you into a dither for the entire weekend," Darbie said.

"I say we go on with the film," Fiona said.

"We can meet at my house tomorrow for the whole day," Darbie said.

They were all looking at Sophie as if the next words out of her mouth would decide whether they gave up on life as they knew it. Kitty's face was the most hopeful.

"I love you guys," Sophie said.

"We're the best, the best, the best," Kitty said. Her voice cracked as she threw her arms around Sophie. "I don't know how I would stand it right now if it weren't for you."

After that, how could Sophie even think about Miss Imes or detention or what Daddy was going to say?

Sophie, Fiona, Willoughby, and Maggie went to Darbie's that night and slept over, although Kitty's mom didn't let her come until the next morning. The Corn Flakes all promised her that they wouldn't have a bit of fun before she got there. They did, but they tried not to talk about that in front of Kitty when they were finally all together eating Darbie's aunt Emily's pancakes. They already had a movie name for her when she got there, though—the maiden Katrina.

Maggie, it had also been decided the night before, was Maid Magdalena the Dark.

Darbie was named Lady Patricia the Irish, and Willoughby chose just plain Willow. She started making up medieval cheers about her character immediately.

The only possible name for Fiona was Lady of the Rapier. She said a "rapier" was a slender sword with two edges so it could cut both ways. That's how sharp the Rapier's wit would be.

Sophie, naturally, was Aurora.

"Aurora the Mighty," Kitty said. She giggled, but the trust in her blue eyes made Sophie feel like she just might *be* mighty.

Once they got started acting out scenes and Maggie wrote them into the script, the Corn Flakes killed themselves—*killed* themselves—laughing all day. They stayed true to their Code, which didn't allow for anything that could hurt somebody's feelings or be mean. So when they came up with things like, "Excuse me, but have you a large fly on your nose? Oh, I'm sorry—that's a wart!" they crossed them out. But the jokes were really hard to part with.

Fiona kept their literature and history books open in front of her and Darbie's computer constantly online so she could keep the film medieval-accurate. She was the one who came up with the need for a jousting tournament scene, where four of the maidens thrust wrapping-paper rolls at dummies of villains and vixens they constructed from stacks of pillows. They shouted their best one-liners while the rescued maiden Katrina clapped and threw roses at the winner.

Maggie got it all with Sophie's camera, and when they crowded around its little digital window to see their work, Kitty laughed so hard, Sophie thought she was going to lose her breath. It wasn't the noble, serious film Sophie had imagined. But if it meant Kitty could have something to look forward to besides more chemotherapy and more throwing up and more being too tired to play, it couldn't be goofy enough.

Sophie *had* to keep that camera. That was why, when she was back home in her own bed that night, she remembered Miss Imes and Coach Yates. She couldn't think of anything funny OR noble that she would be capable of to deal with them. Or to keep Mama and Daddy from finding out. It was an old feeling—that one she used to get, long before she met Fiona and before the Corn Flakes started. Long before she met Dr. Peter and learned to imagine Jesus. It was a heavy feeling that meant, *I CAN'T do this. I CAN'T!*

The hippo-sized lump reappeared in her throat. Praying. Imagining Jesus. She wasn't doing any of that these days. How could she make sure Kitty knew him when she herself felt like he was now living in another town?

Sophie closed her eyes and tried to see Jesus with his kind eyes. The Jesus who never acted like he had someplace else to be. The Jesus who helped.

It took a long time for her to get a picture of him in her mind. Longer than it ever had before. And when he did come into focus, eyes as kind as ever, Sophie's eyes sprang open.

She couldn't look at him. And she wasn't sure why.

Six

The next morning Mama was too sick to go to Sunday school, and Daddy tried to fix breakfast and get Zeke ready. Except there was no milk in the house and no way to comb Zeke's hair the way Mama did it. Zeke went wearing one of Daddy's ball caps that even covered his nose and hollered about wanting Spider-Man waffles. When they arrived at the church forty-five minutes late, Sophie hung out in the hall outside the Sunday school room because she was too embarrassed to go in so long after class had started. She couldn't shake the feeling that Jesus was very far away—maybe even as far away as the thirteenth century. Dr. Peter found her as he strolled down the corridor with a cup of coffee.

"Sophie-Lophie-Loodle!" he said. He shot a puzzled look at the classroom door.

"I'm too late," Sophie said.

"You're looking a little—what does Fiona always say?" He chuckled. "Vexed. Are you vexed?"

Yes! Sophie wanted to say. *I feel like I went off someplace and left Jesus, and now I can't look at him because I know he's not happy with me and I don't even know why—*

And yet even as Dr. Peter waited quietly, sipping his coffee and steaming up his glasses, she couldn't say any of it. There was just too much crowding to get out.

"You don't *have* to talk about it," Dr. Peter said.

"Do you think Jesus has a sense of humor?" Sophie blurted out.

Dr. Peter stopped in mid-sip and blinked. "Well," he said, "when we think of God and Jesus as one, sure—I mean, God has to have a sense of what's funny to create a rhinoceros—or my hair." He patted his curls, all gelled down for Sunday.

Sophie shook her head. "I mean, like, did Jesus ever say funny things to get people to think or, like, make them back off and stop being stupid?"

Dr. Peter took a really long drink out of his cup and said, "There isn't anything like that in the Gospel stories. But, then, we don't know everything he said when he wasn't busy teaching and healing and all that ..."

Sophie looked down at her boot tops and up through the bill of her denim ball cap, everywhere but at Dr. Peter. It was the first time ever that she didn't want him to see what was in her eyes.

The door to the middle school room opened, and the Corn Flakes and the two Wheaties burst out. They surrounded Sophie and Dr. Peter with questions and squeals and the need to display Kitty in a trucker hat with "I Love Jesus" embroidered on it.

"My dad bought it for me to wear when I go back in the hospital Wednesday for my chemo," she said. "It'll make me feel like I'm with you guys."

"Back in the hospital?" Sophie said. Her heart was already pounding and heading for her throat.

"I like the hat," Dr. Peter said to Kitty.

"I think we should all get them," Darbie said.

"But not shave our heads," Willoughby whispered to Sophie while the rest of the girls went on chattering. "The Pops are giving me enough trouble without that."

"How come you didn't tell us?" Sophie said.

Willoughby shrugged. "My problems aren't as bad as Kitty's," she said. "They're not talking to me at cheerleading practice, and every time I make a suggestion, they just act like I didn't even say anything. The girls who didn't go through elementary with us act like they're afraid of the Pops, so they ignore me too. *Plus*, Cassie is there watching every practice, and she's always pointing at me and rolling her eyes." Willoughby hugged Sophie's arm. "I try to just laugh, but it's hard when you're not there."

"All right," Dr. Peter said, "who's working on the Bible study assignment?"

"Me!" Kitty said.

Everybody else nodded too, and Sophie bobbed her head right along with them. But she was careful to keep her eyes away from Dr. Peter's.

I WILL do it, she thought. *Just as soon as I find out what it is!*

As soon as the worship service was over, Fiona dragged Sophie aside.

"Did you tell your dad about needing help in math yet?" she said.

"No," Sophie said. "He might take the camera away from me right now, and we don't have that much time left with Kitty."

"Don't worry about it," Fiona said. "I'm gonna go in before school tomorrow and convince Miss Imes that I'm the absolutely best tutor you could ever have and that you will totally ace the next quiz with my help." Her magic-gray eyes were shining. "I'll sit there until she sees it my way."

"You would do that?" Sophie said.

"Hello! I'm your best friend."

"I wish you knew a way to get me out of detention," Sophie said.

Fiona's eyes shone. "You'll make Coach Hates see how awesome you are, Soph. You always end up doing that."

Sophie couldn't even nod.

"I think I totally won Miss Imes over," Fiona told Sophie during PE the next day.

But before Sophie could even start to hope, Coach Yates yelled, "LaCroix! Don't forget you have detention after school Wednesday."

Sophie realized something she hadn't before, something that made things even worse. "Does it have to be Wednesday?" she said. "I have Bible study after school on Wednesdays. Could I come in during lunch or something?"

Coach Yates looked down at her, face ponytail-pinched. "Bible study?" she said. "I don't think it's doing you any good, LaCroix—not the way you keep pushing everything. Wednesday's the only day I hold detention. Be here, or expect an F in citizenship. Now, give me six laps."

Sophie couldn't catch up with the other Flakes, and Coach Yates barked at them when she saw them slowing down. So Sophie ran around the track six times alone, until her side felt like it had been stabbed and her thoughts were in a tangle.

At least I won't have to have my Bible assignment done, not that I even know what it is. And Mama is REALLY gonna be upset that I have to miss Bible study because I got in trouble. Mama? What about Daddy?

Not only that, but Kitty was going to leave, and then Sophie wouldn't have her to think about instead of all the other stuff. And what if Kitty didn't get all the things she needed to know about Jesus and she got more sick and—Sophie pulled away from that thought and went to, *I'm going to be the only one with a bald head in the whole school now.*

But that's not what's important.

Then why did she get that big lump in her throat when the Pops called her Little Boy LaCroix?

Sophie didn't feel any closer to untangling that knotted mess when she got to math class. She pulled off her blue-knit twirl cap as she walked into the room and went to her desk without even looking at a Corn Pop or a Fruit Loop, just in case one of them wanted to start in. But before she could sit down, Miss Imes said to her, "I'm putting you in the back with your tutor."

At least she was keeping her voice low. Sophie was grateful for that. And being in the last row with Fiona was going to make life way better.

"Tod Ravelli will be working with you," Miss Imes said.

Sophie's mouth fell open so far she could taste chalk dust.

"*Tod?*" Sophie said.

Miss Imes whipped off her half-glasses. Her eyebrows threatened to shoot right off her face. "If there is any more arguing, I will assume you don't want help, and I will be on the telephone to your parents."

Sophie couldn't even get out a "Yes, ma'am." She just nodded and struggled to swallow the hippopotamus that was in her throat again. She collected her backpack and made her way blindly to the back of the room. Out of the corner of her eye, she could see Fiona waving her hand to be called on.

"It's a done deal, Fiona," Miss Imes said.

Tod joined Sophie after a quick conference with Miss Imes, all tough and swaggering, winking at Julia as he passed her.

Why isn't he saying he doesn't want to sit with me? Sophie thought. He was up to something.

Tod plopped himself into the next desk and scooted it closer to Sophie. She tried not to shudder.

"So where's your book, Soapy?" he said.

Sophie was careful not to take her eyes off him as she pulled out her math book. He slouched against the back of the chair and made a big *L* on his forehead with his thumb and index finger for Colton's benefit. Colton made one back.

But Sophie could feel somebody else staring at her. Julia. Her green eyes seemed to be made of steel at the moment as she bored them into Tod. He looked at her and whispered, "What?"

He's stupider than I thought, Sophie said to herself. *She's mad because he's sitting so close to me, and he can't even see that.*

"All right, class, Sophie and Tod are not on display for your entertainment," Miss Imes said. "Eyes this way, please."

As the class turned reluctantly to the board, Fiona gave Sophie one last glance that clearly said, *Don't be mad at me. I really tried.*

"So, like, I'm gonna teach you some shortcuts."

Sophie stared at Tod. She could smell grape gum on his breath.

"Why?" she said.

"Because the faster you get it, the faster I don't have to sit back here with you anymore."

That was the first familiar thing that had happened all day, and Sophie grabbed at it.

"I want to get that done, like, yesterday," she said.

Tod poked at a problem on the open page of his book with his pencil. "I'll show you how to do this one *way* easier than the way Imes explains it. All you do is— "

Tod completed the problem in three short steps. Sophie stared at it.

"You don't even get *that*?" Tod said.

"I get it," Sophie said. She blinked. "It just can't be that easy."

"Don't believe me then. Just keep flunking."

"No!" Sophie said. "I'll try it."

She wrote down the numbers, followed Tod's steps, and came up with an answer.

"Right?" she said.

"Dude," Tod said. "You're not as dumb as everybody says you are."

"Give me another one," Sophie said.

He did. She worked it, and she got it right.

After five more correct answers, the hippo in Sophie's throat started to swim off somewhere. But then she caught it by the tail.

"How come you know the easy way and Miss Imes doesn't?" Sophie said.

Tod gave her a pointy look. "She knows it—duh. But she's a teacher. She has to make it hard, or they don't pay her."

"So I guess you aren't getting paid," Sophie said.

"Like she's really gonna give me cash," Tod said. He leaned in even closer. Sophie could practically feel Julia stabbing her in the temple with her eyes. "But if you don't pass the next test, I get a D in citizenship. I forgot to tell you that part."

"When did you start caring about your citizenship grade?" Sophie said.

"When I found out you can't play sports if you get below a B. Stupid rule. Anyways, you gotta pass the quiz, so do ten more of these just like I showed you, and I'll tell you if you get the right answers."

Sophie gnawed at her eraser. It was way hard to trust Tod. When had he ever done anything for a Corn Flake?

But one thing they all knew: the Fruit Loops practically breathed sports. If Tod wasn't going to be able to play football or something because she failed, he was going to make sure she didn't.

Besides, not being a total moron on a math problem felt, as Fiona would say, blissful. That day, and the next day too.

Seven

Tod is still a heinous creature," Sophie told the Flakes at their Tuesday afternoon movie rehearsal at Fiona's house. "But he's really teaching me. I'm SO gonna pass that math quiz tomorrow."

"Will you call me in the hospital and tell me?" Kitty said. She was sitting listlessly on top of a pile of cushions, pulling the petals off the silk rose she was holding.

"I will call you every day and tell you every single detail," Sophie said.

"I'll email you," Fiona said. "We have a high-speed Internet connection."

Kitty pulled out three petals at once. "But I want to be *here*. And what about our movie?"

Sophie could barely talk over the lump in her throat, but she managed to say, "That's why we're filming all your parts today—so you won't miss anything."

"Let's do it with the hats on," Darbie said. "That'll be class!"

Maggie pulled out the cone-shaped hats her mom, who always made their costumes, had put together. They were all covered in shiny couch-like material and had trailing chiffon veils. With those on their heads, the jousting tournament scene came alive, although they were definitely going to need a way to keep them in place. Darbie took the point of Maggie's right in the armpit when it flew off. Nobody could stop laughing. Especially not Kitty.

"Do you promise you'll send me a DVD when it's all finished?" Kitty said. Her blue eyes were filmy.

I HAVE to get everything fixed so I can keep the camera, Sophie thought fiercely. *And I will.*

"Okay, Maggie," she said. "Let's shoot that scene again—"

For the first time in her whole seventh-grade experience, Sophie was looking forward to going to math class Wednesday. By that time, she had imagined over and over the look on Miss Imes's face when she saw all the problems done right on Sophie's paper, and now she was going to *see* it.

And, Sophie thought, Miss Imes was going to see Aurora/Sophie, the girl who didn't act out on purpose, the girl who only wanted to protect her friends from villains and vixens without becoming one herself.

In fact, that seemed to be working. Nobody had picked on them for two days, except for what Willoughby was going through at practice. And even though that was Corn Pop-heinous, at least they had a new mission. It made being without Kitty a little easier.

Protecting Willoughby is our next challenge, Sophie decided. *Right after I ace this test.*

It was with the confidence of Aurora herself that Sophie attacked her math quiz, brandishing her sword—pencil. She was one of the first people to turn hers in, right behind Tod.

"Hey, Miz I," Tod said.

"Yes, Mr. R," Miss Imes said.

"Would you grade Soapy's right now so I can see how she did?"

Miss Imes's eyebrows pointed up. "'Soapy'?" she said.

To Sophie's horror, Tod flung his arm around her shoulders. "That's my pet name for her," he said.

His skin was clammy on her neck, and Sophie couldn't help gasping. She was pretty sure she heard Julia gasp too.

"Have a seat, Romeo," Miss Imes said in a dry voice. "And I'll call you up when I've checked your paper."

Sophie was barely back in her desk when Miss Imes scraped her chair back and called Sophie's name as she charged for the door. Sophie followed her out, and Miss Imes shut the door behind her. The teacher's whole face seemed to be pointing upward.

"What is *this*?" Miss Imes said.

She held up Sophie's quiz. There was a large red F at the top. Sophie was sure her heart stopped.

"I thought you were paying attention to Tod," Miss Imes said.

Sophie shook her head as she stared at her paper. She had never felt more bald.

"I did listen to him!" she said. "And after he showed me the easy way to do the problems, I've been getting all the answers right!"

Miss Imes pulled another paper out from behind Sophie's. It was Tod's, and it had a huge A+ on it.

"Tod got all the answers correct. You got none of them right. Obviously, you didn't do it the way he showed you."

Sophie pulled her face closer to Tod's paper. "*He* didn't do it the way he showed me!"

"Are you saying he taught you wrong?" Miss Imes said.

"No—he wouldn't do that because—!"

"Because he obviously likes you. The whole nickname thing—"

"It's not that!" Sophie said. Her voice, she knew, was going so high it was almost off the scale. "If I don't pass, he gets a D in citizenship, and then he can't play sports!"

Miss Imes took off her half-glasses and drilled her eyes into Sophie's. "Where on earth did you get an idea like that?"

"Tod told me," Sophie said.

"I would never put that kind of responsibility on a student. Are you sure you heard him right?"

Sophie's shoulders nearly met in the middle. "I should have known," she said. It was only the hippo in her throat that kept her from crying. Her voice barely came out.

"Should have known what?" Miss Imes said.

"That he would try to trick me—but I didn't think he'd think of something like that—I bet it was Julia or Anne-Stuart who thought of it—"

Sophie stopped herself and listened to the Code shatter to the ground. She bit her lip, and wished she could bite back the rest of it.

Miss Imes crossed her arms, the quizzes still dangling from one hand along with her glasses.

"So," Miss Imes said, "there's some sort of war going on among you kids?"

"It's their war, not ours," Sophie said.

"And do you really think this is the way to fight it?" Miss Imes glanced again at Sophie's quiz. "You can't pull it off the way your friends do. Fiona, Darbie, Maggie, Willoughby, even poor little Kitty—they're all managing to keep their math grades up while they're following you around stirring things up with a stick."

"All we want," Sophie managed to say, "is for people not to harass other people. Especially Kitty."

"I'm just not seeing anybody doing any harassing. All I've seen is you clowning around in my class." Miss Imes put her glasses back on and looked over the quizzes yet again. "It really is your word against Tod's though," she said. She sighed. "I'll look into it. In the meantime, here's what we're going to do. I am going to allow you to retake the quiz tomorrow. If you pass, I will throw this quiz away. I trust you'll be getting help from Fiona outside of class, since Tod obviously didn't do the job."

"But you said Fiona couldn't be my tutor."

There was another sigh. "Just because I said you couldn't work with Fiona in class doesn't mean you can't seek her help outside. I don't understand why you didn't do that before things got this bad for you. Although I suppose you two can't settle down to anything together anytime except to joke your way through your 'war.'"

"I'm dumb in math!" Sophie cried. "And there's a Code, and I can't break it—but I have to protect—"

She stopped, because the words were coming out in pieces all chopped up by sobs. She knew she wasn't making any sense.

Miss Imes pulled a tissue out of her sleeve and handed it to her. "Use this until you get to the restroom to wash your face," she said. Her voice was a little softer. "Go ahead and have the rest of your cry while you're in there."

Sophie nodded. She could hardly see as she turned to go.

"Sophie."

Sophie stopped and waited, but she didn't look back.

"Just be honest," Miss Imes said. "Then maybe we can get somewhere."

Why? Sophie thought as she half-ran to the girls' restroom. *You wouldn't believe me anyway.*

Aurora choked back her tears as she leaned against the castle wall. There was no time to cry. And there was no time to defend herself. There was only the crusade—to stop the villains and vixens—

But all the Codes in the world didn't seem to be enough. For the first time in her life as a mighty maiden of the Court, she felt unable to defend herself.

Sophie stayed in the restroom until class was over. She didn't want to see Tod and the rest of them looking all innocent and disgusting. The Flakes would be waiting for her, and they would figure something out over lunch.

My maidens! The thought was like a shaft of light coming into Aurora's heart. They will be waiting there for me, and they will vouch for my character. I have taught them well!

All of them were pulled into a knot at the end of the math hall when Sophie got there. And even Fiona was white-faced.

"It's okay," Sophie said. She attempted a smile. "Tod taught me wrong, and she's going to let me take the test over— "

"She did take him out in the hall," Darbie said. But she didn't really look at Sophie.

"What's going on?" Sophie said.

"Miss Imes yelled at us," Fiona said.

"She didn't exactly yell," Maggie said. "She just said we would all be in trouble if we kept 'doing battle.' " Maggie's face darkened. "Even if the stuff we did wasn't against the rules in the handbook."

"Um, you guys?" They all turned to Willoughby. She looked like an egg about to crack open. "I have to go," she said. And she took off running.

"*What?*" Sophie said.

"She's afraid she's gonna get kicked off the cheerleading squad if she gets in trouble," Maggie said. "She's probably right."

Sophie's throat got thick as she watched Willoughby's retreating figure. "What did you tell Miss Imes?"

"Nothing," Fiona said. "What was the point in arguing?"

"Because I'm in trouble!" Sophie said. "She thinks I'm the biggest liar and troublemaker on the planet, but she would have believed it if you'd told her I wasn't!"

"If we argued with her, that would only make it worse." Fiona drew closer to Sophie, and so did the rest of them. "It's okay, Soph. We're still gonna do what we've been doing. We just have to be careful not to do it in front of her, or you'll get your camera taken away and we won't be able to make movies and— "

"I can't, Sophie," Darbie said. "I can't!"

Sophie looked at Darbie in time to see her face crumple. Her knees sagged, and Sophie knew she would have dropped right down to the floor if Maggie hadn't caught her.

"It was fine when we were just playing and making flicks," Darbie said between globby sobs, "but when she started talking about war—I got scared. I've seen enough war— "

A door opened down the hall, and everyone stiffened.

"Come on," Maggie whispered as she lifted Darbie up by her armpits. "We *are* gonna get in trouble if we keep standing here."

Fiona and Maggie swept Darbie off to the cafeteria. But Sophie didn't follow them.

When she had stared at their backs until they disappeared, she threw her lunch into the first trashcan she found and went to the outside courtyard and sat on a bench.

Could I get in trouble for THIS too? she thought. She pulled herself into a ball.

How come everything is suddenly about not getting in trouble? I thought we were all about the Code—

I cannot be discouraged, Aurora told herself. *They have all run like frightened rabbits, and there is nothing to laugh about now—no Spirit of Mirth. But I must be strong.*

She ran her hand across the smooth scalp she had been so happy to shave—for the Code. It had been a drastic move, one she had never expected Willow or Magdalena or Patricia or even her faithful Rapier to make for the maiden Katrina. But she had never regretted it, even now that Katrina was gone and no longer needed their protection.

"I would do the same for any of them!" she cried. "I would do anything to defend the Code we have worked so hard to form! I would march right up to any villain—"

From afar a bell tolled. Sophie only shook herself out of Aurora's world long enough to get to science class and settle in her seat. Just as she was about to return to her vow to uphold the Code against any odds, a folded piece of paper appeared on her desk

"We'll be moving to the lab in just a few minutes," Mr. Stires said in his always-cheerful voice. "I want you to get out two sheets of paper and a pencil and be ready—"

Sophie opened the note, folded into an origami bird as only Fiona did it, and read: *Are you mad at us? Please don't be.*

Sophie looked up at Fiona, who was blinking like a kitten from over the top of her backpack. She didn't even have time to say yes or no before Mr. Stires began herding them into the lab area.

How can I be angry with you, my friend? Aurora thought. *I would die for you! I would march up to any villain and face him dead-on before I would abandon you to his evils—*

Even as the thoughts galloped through Aurora's mind on gallant steeds, she caught sight of one of the smaller villains, the Ridiculous Tod of Loop Land. He had a javelin in his hand, and as he pulled his

arm back, Aurora knew he meant ill will. Plunging forth through a crowd of innocent members of the court, she dived for the now-flying spear and caught it in midair. Clutching it to her bosom—which was larger than any other maiden's in the kingdom—she crumpled to the ground with the skirts of her gown piled around her—

"I'm glad you're so enthusiastic," Mr. Stires said. "But there's no need to knock yourself out getting there. We'll wait for you."

Sophie scrambled to her feet. Miss Imes said all the teachers were saying things about her. Maybe even happy Mr. Stires.

Only when Sophie was standing up again did she realize she was holding a paper airplane that looked like it had been folded and unfolded a bunch of times. She glanced around. Where had it come from?

As soon as she got to her lab station, Sophie unfolded it. There were several different colors of ink used in as many different handwritings. Sophie recognized Anne-Stuart's curlicue letters as the first one.

WE'VE GOT THAT BUNCH OF GOOD GIRLS NOW, she had written.

ONE MORE TO GO AND THEY'RE DONE, somebody else had added.

IT'S GONNA BE SO EASY. THEY'RE NOTHING WITHOUT LBL, said the next one.

YEAH, BUT WE STILL HAVE TO WATCH HER.

THEY WILL GO DOWN.

DO IT FOR CASSIE.

"Let's get started," Mr. Stires sang out.

Sophie stuffed the note into the pocket of her jeans and tried to concentrate on the making-cotton-candy lab. It was hard with the words shouting in her head: *ONE MORE TO GO AND THEY'RE DONE.*

The Good Girls, that's us, she thought. *Who else would it be?*

THEY'RE NOTHING WITHOUT LBL, one of them had said. That was her, she knew—Little Boy LaCroix. *So they really did plan that whole thing so I'd be scared to get in more trouble with Miss Imes*, she thought. *They even got Tod in on it.*

But who was the ONE MORE TO GO?

Eight

It didn't take long to find out. At the end of science class, an announcement was made over the intercom for all cheerleaders to come to the office.

"Our uniforms are here!" Anne-Stuart said.

She bounced toward the door, corn-silk hair flying, before the bell even rang, and latched on to Julia on the way out.

"B.J.!" Julia shouted in the direction of the hallway. "Wait up!"

Sophie got to the doorway just as the three of them took off down the hall, squealing. And leaving Willoughby in their dust. Sophie watched her try to catch up, everything on her drooping as she fell farther behind.

"Why didn't they wait for you, Willoughby?" somebody called out.

It was Cassie, using the Corn Pop I'm-your-friend-right-now voice.

Willoughby just walked faster, legs stiff. But Julia, now about to turn the corner in the hall, whipped her head around with a toss of her ponytail, and called back, "Oh, sor-ry, Willoughby. We forgot about *you*." With another toss she was gone.

Sophie felt a nudge on her arm as Fiona pushed her in the other direction. "We can't be late to sixth period if all the teachers are gonna be holding surveillance on us."

Sophie didn't even ask her what *surveillance* meant. She was too busy watching Darbie work her way through the hallway crowd ahead of them like a burrowing dachshund.

I can't do it, Sophie! Darbie had said.

Sophie followed Fiona, bumped by elbows and backpacks and unhappy thoughts.

Who IS going to do it, then?

The Pops were after Willoughby because she made cheerleader instead of Cassie. Would Aurora just let it go because teachers didn't understand?

"No!" Aurora cried. Her noble, womanly arm came up, fist clenched in the air. "I will uphold the Code, even if I have to do it alone!"

Alone? You never have to do it alone. Listen to me—

"Hey, get off me, Cue Ball!"

Sophie stumbled forward, one leg tangled in Colton Messik's too-big pant leg. She could feel them both going down—until something grabbed at the straps of her backpack and yanked her back to her feet. Colton, who was still staggering around to get his balance, looked up and said, "Hey, Coach. How's it going?"

"Get up, Messik," said a familiar high-pitched-for-a-man voice.

Sophie closed her eyes and prepared to die. Coach Virile. He was still holding on to her straps, and Sophie could feel his one big eyebrow looming over her.

"Thanks," she said without looking up at him. Maybe he wouldn't recognize her.

"Let's get to class, people. And try not to kill each other while you're doing it."

Everybody else scattered like ants, which Sophie would have loved to do if Coach Virile wasn't holding her captive. Even when he let go as the hall emptied, she didn't move.

"For such a little thing you sure get yourself into some big messes, don't you?" he said.

"I don't try to," she said to the floor.

"Hey."

It was a command to look at him. Sophie obeyed. Just as she'd suspected, his eyebrow was hooding his face. But his eyes weren't poking at her like pencil points this time. They looked surprised. He folded his arms, like two large hams.

"You okay?" he said.

Sophie couldn't answer. Coach Virile hunched his shoulders to get closer to her level. "If somebody's giving you trouble," he said, "don't go it alone. There are people here who can — "

Sophie didn't hear the rest. *Don't go it alone. That* drowned everything else out.

"Coach Yates," Coach Virile was now calling into the Life Skills classroom. "I held this one up. You mind if I have a minute with Colton Messik?"

"Please," Coach Yates said, "and any of the rest of them you want to take off my hands."

A few minutes later, Willoughby, Julia, Anne-Stuart, and B.J. returned. The Pops looked like they'd just been to Disney World. Willoughby looked like she was coming back from a year at the state prison. Sophie kept her eyes on the Pops. Julia nodded to Anne-Stuart, who turned around to look at Cassie. A sly smile appeared on Anne-Stuart's face, and as she tilted her head ever so slightly toward Willoughby, she turned a thumb up for Cassie to see.

Thank you, Cassie mouthed to her.

A sizzle went through Aurora's veins. The vixens were trying to take Willow down, remove her from the Dance. But what could she do now? Everyone was watching, waiting for Aurora to make a false move. Even the maidens were too frightened to act. Could she go it alone?

That word rankled like a chain in her mind. It wasn't a word she was accustomed to. And now she was hearing it from unexpected places.

Aurora raised her head. There was no time to ponder that now. If she was going to know what to do for Willow, she needed more information. And there was only one way to get it.

The bell rang, and Sophie headed for the door with a purpose. Coach Yates stopped her with a different one.

"I'll see you in ten minutes in my office, LaCroix," she said.

Outside in the hall, Sophie leaned against the wall and tried to think. The Flakes stood around her.

"You couldn't talk her out of it, huh?" Fiona said. Her voice seemed stiff.

"Does your mom know?" Maggie said.

Sophie shook her head. "You guys go ahead with—who's driving today?"

"Aunt Emily," Darbie said. She was already backing away.

"I'm not going. I have cheerleading," Willoughby said. "Ms. Hess said we can't miss any practices before the assembly Monday."

Sophie felt an idea forming. "The rest of you just go," she said, "and I'll take the last bus home and tell Mama then."

Willoughby was watching Sophie closely. "You sure are calm about it. I'd be bawling my eyes out."

"It'll be okay," Sophie said.

Heads nodded woodenly. Sophie only let herself feel a little bit of a sting as she watched them go. Then she pulled herself up to what height she could reach and marched off to detention. If it worked out the way she hoped, it could be a very good thing for the maidens and their Code.

The cheerleaders were all changing into their shorts and tennies when Sophie passed through the locker room on her way to Coach Yates' office. So far, so good.

When Coach Yates told her she had to go up and down the bleachers in the gym and pick up trash, that was a plus as well.

Just as Willoughby had told them she always did, Cassie was sitting in the bleachers, twisting her long, very-straight hair around her hand and watching wistfully as the cheerleaders gathered for practice.

It is an excellent plan, Aurora said to herself. I cannot hold back.

So Sophie snapped open the big black garbage bag Coach Yates had given her and zipped up and down her assigned rows of bleachers, collecting discarded handouts and empty candy wrappers and broken pencils. It left the other detention-ites looking like slackers.

She made absolutely sure she had covered her whole area before she went back to clean up the row where Cassie was sitting. Then she became so slow and thorough, Mr. Clean himself could have come in behind her with a white glove.

When Sophie got within a few feet of Cassie, she ran her hand under the bench in front of her and made a disgusted noise.

"How foul is that?" she said.

"What?" Cassie said.

"Big old nasty wad of gum," Sophie said. "That's just disgusting."

"Do you have to get it off?" Cassie said. She curled back her lip, blue braces showing.

"Yeah," Sophie said. "Don't ever get detention."

"I don't plan to," Cassie said.

Her eyes returned to the Pops, who weren't cheering but standing in a bunch squabbling. The girls Sophie didn't know were huddled a little apart from them. Sophie forced herself not to search out Willoughby.

I might not be able to go through with it if I see her crying, she thought.

"It doesn't sound like it's going so well," Sophie said, as she pretended to scrape off the nonexistent wad of gum with her thumbnail.

"It would be if Willoughby could actually cheer," Cassie said. Then she darted her eyes to Sophie. "I know she's your friend, but she totally can't do the moves."

"Really?" Sophie said. She chose her words carefully. *No lying*, she told herself. *Just get Cassie talking.*

"Haven't you been watching?" Cassie said. "It's not even that hard, but she's all falling down and stuff."

Sophie shrugged. "I don't know that much about cheering. You saw me at the tryouts."

Cassie snorted. "Why did you try out anyway?" she said, curling her lip again. Julia, Sophie decided, had really been working with her.

"Just for fun," Sophie said. "And so Willoughby wouldn't be nervous."

There was another snort. "If she was that nervous at tryouts, how is she ever gonna stand up in front of the whole school and cheer Monday at the assembly? Of course she'll mess up. We'll make sure— "

Cassie stopped. Sophie glanced up to see her narrow face flush.

"You think she'll mess up?" Sophie said.

Cassie turned toward the gym floor where Ms. Hess had arrived. The group was finally lined up, hands on hips. When the music started, they went into their routine, arms in perfect straight lines, voices husky, hips making circles over their fast-moving feet. Sophie had to admit, she was impressed with the way they were all in time with each other, as if the same puppeteer were moving them all. Including Willoughby.

"Willoughby looks good to me," Sophie said to Cassie.

"Yeah, well—just wait 'til Monday. She's going to look like a moron."

Sophie looked at Cassie, who had her eyes glued on the cheerleaders. Eyes that gleamed like tomorrow was Christmas.

"So she looks good now, but she's going to look like a moron Monday," Sophie said. "Okay—whatever."

Cassie's mouth opened, and then she gave Sophie a sharp look. "Aren't you and Willoughby really close?" she said.

Sophie sucked in air. This was the hard part—the part where she had to decide.

"You guys *are* close," Cassie said. Her words were like accusing fingers. "You're like best friends."

"Not so much," Sophie said. "In fact, Willoughby isn't talking to me as much now, not since lunchtime today."

That's not a total lie, she shouted at herself. *I can't help her if I don't do this!*

Cassie nodded. "Julia and them said she's that way. They said she used to hang out with them all the time, and then she just dumped them and started being friends with y'all."

"Uh-huh," Sophie said.

"It's totally going to bite her in the behind Monday," Cassie said, "when she makes an idiot out of herself at the assembly and Ms. Hess takes her off the squad."

Sophie picked up her garbage bag and nodded. She climbed down the bleachers, and over her shoulder she lied again: "Nice talking to you, Cassie."

Sophie turned in her garbage bag to Coach Yates and promised she would be on time to every class and not try to entertain everybody anymore. Coach Yates didn't exactly look convinced. Sophie tried not to think about that as she went to a bench out front to wait for the late bus. She had to think about Willoughby.

So now I know they're trying to make Willoughby mess up at the assembly so Ms. Hess will take her off the squad and put Cassie on. But HOW are they going to do it?

Sophie didn't care what Cassie Corn Pop said. Willoughby knew that routine like she was born doing it.

She had to find out their plan. And the only way to do that was to stay as close as she could to the Pops and gather information.

That isn't gonna look TOO suspicious! Sophie thought. *They're gonna know I'm up to something—unless—*

Sophie shook her head, nearly knocking off her cap. She'd already made Cassie think she and Willoughby weren't that close anymore, and it didn't feel good.

What felt worse was that maybe it wasn't a lie. The Flakes had been too scared to stand up for her with Miss Imes, and they'd acted all stiff and weird after school. Even though Sophie almost understood, it made her feel coldly alone.

"We are not alone," Aurora said. "Just like King Arthur, we are forgetting something very important."

"Hey, Soapy— "

That definitely wasn't it.

"Hey, Cue Ball— "

Sophie looked at a wall of smiling faces that didn't usually smile at her.

"Stop calling her lame names, y'all," Julia said. "We've outgrown that."

"Not only that— " B.J. gave Tod a shove, which landed him almost in Sophie's lap, which set Colton and Eddie off into boy-steria, which made Julia say, "To-od—make them quit!" It stopped only when Tod punched Eddie in the stomach.

Anne-Stuart sat down next to Sophie, her pale blue eyes wide and serious. "Cassie said y'all were talking during cheerleading practice."

Careful, Sophie told herself. "Uh-huh," she said.

Julia joined her on the other side. "She told you that Willoughby is going to mess up at the assembly when we do our cheer."

"And we totally know you're gonna go tell her— " B.J. started to say.

"Shut UP!" the rest of them shouted at her.

Anne-Stuart put her hand on Sophie's arm. Sophie imagined it rotting her skin.

"Willoughby's going to mess up on her own," Anne-Stuart said. "We aren't going to make her."

Julia tossed her ponytail. "We don't even want her to. We just know she will. And if you tell her what Cassie said, she'll just be all nervous and mess up worse and then we'll *all* look bad."

And we wouldn't want THAT now, would we? Sophie wanted to say to her. But she waited. She could tell there was more by the way B.J. was holding on to Tod, who was edging away like he had to go to the bathroom.

"I know we all used to hate each other," Julia went on. "Your friends and ours."

When did that change? Sophie thought.

"But we think that's immature now," Anne-Stuart said. "Especially what Tod did to you in math."

She sniffed up a nose-full in B.J.'s direction, and B.J. thrust Tod forward again. He stopped just short of Sophie's toes.

"You're busted, man!" Colton said. Eddie clapped like an ape.

"Shut UP!" Tod said.

"Tell her, Tod," Julia said.

Tod crossed his arms and smirked at Sophie. "I'm sorry you got messed up on the test. I didn't teach you that good."

"Hel-lo!" Sophie said. "You told me the wrong way to do it on purpose!"

"I was just messing around," Tod said.

"But he's sorry now," Julia said. "And he wants to teach you the right way so you'll do good on the re-test."

"Why?" Sophie said.

The Pops looked at each other. Tod looked at them. Colton and Eddie just looked like they were bored.

"Well," Julia said. "It's like you do us a favor and we do you a favor. Instead of fighting all the time."

"So let me get this straight," Sophie said. "I do you a favor by not telling Willoughby that you think she's gonna mess up at the assembly so she won't get all nervous and really mess up—and you do me a favor by helping me pass the test that Tod made me fail in the first place."

There was another exchange of looks, and then Julia said, "Yeah. That's basically it."

Sophie would have laughed at them if something hadn't been niggling in the back of her mind. There was a hole the Pops and the Loops obviously didn't see.

"Okay," Sophie said. "If I make an A on the re-test, I won't tell Willoughby."

"An A?" Tod said. "It'll never happen."

"Then I guess the deal's off," Sophie said.

She started to get up, but Julia grabbed her sleeve. "Tod will make sure you ace it," she said, never taking her green eyes off him. "Right, baby?"

"I'm gonna puke!" Eddie said.

For the first time ever, Sophie had to agree with him. But Tod just nodded.

"He'll call you tonight, Sophie," Anne-Stuart said.

"One more thing," Julia said in a low voice. "When you talk to Tod on the phone tonight, it's just going to be about math, okay?"

"What else would I talk to him about?" Sophie said.

Julia smiled icily. "That's just what I wanted to hear," she said.

Nine

The late bus pulled up, and Sophie shook the Pops off and headed for it. The hole she'd seen was gaping in her mind: What was to stop her from telling Willoughby that the Pops were definitely up to something—*after* she aced the math test?

And then what was to stop her from keeping her camera and bringing the Flakes back together? There was more to find out, and she was going to. Nothing could stop her now except lack of information.

Nothing except the fact that mothers had some kind of foolproof hotline.

The minute Sophie got inside the kitchen door, Mama dropped a lid on a pot and turned to Sophie with a disappointed face.

"Why didn't you tell me you had detention today?" she said.

Evidently somebody did, Sophie thought. But she couldn't really blame the Flakes. It wasn't part of the Code to lie for each other.

"One thing we've always been able to rely on is your honesty, Soph," Mama said. Her eyes looked so sad, Sophie just wished she'd yell, although she knew she'd be able to count on Daddy for that later.

"This is the truth, Mama," Sophie said. "I kept thinking I could get it changed."

Mama opened the pot and stirred for an endless minute, and then she said, "What did you get detention for?"

Sophie wanted to groan. "I accidentally went into the boys' locker room."

"Were you daydreaming, Soph?"

"That wasn't the reason!" Sophie said.

"Then what was it?" That came from Daddy, who was in the doorway. Sophie didn't even want to know how long he had been there.

Sophie opened her mouth, and then she closed it. *I can't tell DADDY somebody played a joke on me because I'm breast-retarded!* she thought. There had just been too much to deal with that day to go there.

So she looked at the floor and said, "Yeah, I guess maybe that was the reason."

"Then you know what that means," Daddy said.

Sophie nodded miserably. "I'll get it and bring it to you."

But even as Sophie deposited the video camera into Daddy's hands and dragged herself back to her room to flop on her bed, that wasn't what made her want to hurl her glasses across the room and sob into her pillow. It was the sick feeling that flooded over her, that made her refuse spaghetti dinner. Even after she realized that Mama was actually cooking again, she stayed in her room. What if Daddy asked about her grades too? What if she couldn't find out what the Pops were planning for Willoughby? What if her Flakes kept acting stiff and funky?

"Hey, Soph— " Lacie popped her head in the doorway, phone in hand. "It's for you." Her eyes were dancing. "It's a boy," she whispered loudly.

"He's helping me with my math," Sophie said. She snatched the phone from Lacie.

"Why are you getting math help from some absurd little creep?" Lacie said as she exited. "Hel-lo—I'm an algebra whiz!"

Sophie was sure she was going to be sick to her stomach.

"Hello?" she said into the phone.

"It's me," Tod said.

"I know."

"So—I gotta teach you."

Sophie squeezed the receiver. "How do I know you aren't going to mess with me again?"

"Because Miss Imes said if I do, I'm busted."

"You already tried that with me," Sophie said.

"For real this time," Tod said. "She never said I'd get a D in citizenship if you messed up—but she did say I had to try helping you again now. But don't tell Julia I told you that. She thinks I'm doing it for her."

"So start teaching me," Sophie said. "I can't be on the line after nine."

It was hard doing it over the phone, but after about twenty times with the formula that had always escaped her, Sophie finally started getting the problems right.

"Do you swear these are the right answers?" Sophie said when he'd told her she'd gotten three correct in a row.

"Look it up in the back of the book, moron," he said. "All the odd ones are there."

Sophie did. He was right. And so was she.

Just to be on the safe side, when they hung up, Sophie went into Lacie's room to get her to check her work.

"Oh, now you want my help," Lacie said. "Okay—I get it. Boys are cuter than sisters."

Ewww! Sophie wanted to cry. But she forced herself to nod.

Lacie looked over the paper and then up at Sophie. "Nice job, Soph," she said. "Hey, and let me give you a hint about squaring numbers. Here's a trick— "

By the time she was finished, the only thing Sophie could think was: *Why didn't I ask her for help sooner?*

Or Daddy? Or Fiona?

Why did I try to do it by myself? she asked herself as she climbed into bed.

By myself. Alone.

Again.

Sophie closed her eyes, and through the tears that stung at her, she could see each of her Flakes alone too. Kitty in the hospital. Darbie trying to fall asleep with thoughts about war in her head again. Maggie reading the middle-school handbook with a flashlight under the covers, so she wouldn't get in trouble with Miss Imes. Fiona trying to find the right words for it all. Willoughby crying into her pillow—

The tears spilled over. When the door creaked open and Mama tiptoed over to kiss her on the cheek, Sophie pretended she was asleep.

"Soph?" Mama whispered. "Is there something you want to talk about, Dream Girl?"

Sophie stayed still as a stone, and Mama tiptoed back out. Sophie didn't really go to sleep until she made a decision. *I don't want to be alone anymore. Tomorrow I'm going to tell Willoughby BEFORE I even take the test.*

And then I'm going to find out what the Pops are really up to.

And then the Corn Flakes will be okay again.

"Don't forget one thing," Aurora whispered to her—

Whatever it was, it was lost in Sophie's dreams.

The next morning Sophie headed straight to Willoughby's locker, but she barely got to the locker hall before she was surrounded by Corn Pops—minus Cassie.

"Thank you, Sophie," Julia said as she hooked her arm through Sophie's. Anne-Stuart did the same on the other side. B.J. danced in front of them as they made their way toward the stairs.

"For what?" Sophie said. She tried to stop, but her feet were barely touching the ground. "Where are you taking me?"

"Thank you for not trying to get Tod away from me," Julia said. "He said y'all only talked about math."

"Where are we *going*?"

"We're taking you to our place where we always hang out."

"We can talk there," Anne-Stuart said.

"It's way cool," B.J. said. She turned around and led the way down the steps and across the grass toward the gym.

"You can put me down," Sophie said. "I'm not gonna run." No way. This was perfect. She was sure to find out something now that she could tell Willoughby.

But Anne-Stuart and Julia didn't let go of her as they hauled her into the gym and wriggled her and themselves through a space between the bleachers and the wall, which led to an under-the-seats hideaway. Anne-Stuart wafted a hand toward four tumbling mats, arranged in the cracked light like it was somebody's living room.

"Cool, huh?" B.J. said.

"Have a seat," Julia said. B.J. gave Sophie a push that knocked her onto one of the mats. The smiles were gone, and Julia's narrow gaze, striped by the light coming in between the benches, made her look almost cross-eyed.

"I wish the assembly was before the re-test," Julia said. She squatted down in front of Sophie. "But it's not, and that means you could tell Willoughby, now that you know how to do the math problems."

Shameless wenches! Sophie thought. *They figured it out.*

"We have to make sure you don't tell," Anne-Stuart said.

"Okay," Sophie said, shrugging casually. "I won't."

"Not good enough," B.J. said.

Anne-Stuart gave a particularly juicy sniff. "If you tell Willoughby what Cassie blabbed to you, we will tell Miss Imes that we saw you cheating on the re-test."

"How would I cheat?" Sophie said. "I'm the only one taking it!"

"Easy," B.J. said. She was all but licking her chops.

Anne-Stuart pulled a Sharpie out of the front pocket of her backpack. B.J. grabbed Sophie's hand, twisting it until Sophie's palm faced upward.

"Miss Imes will see your cheat sheet right on your hand," Anne-Stuart said as she poised the tip of the Sharpie over Sophie's skin. "What's that formula again, Julia?"

"It's A squared . . ."

Anne-Stuart dug an *A* with a tiny 2 up and to the right of it onto Sophie's palm. Sophie tried to pull away, but B.J. had a grip on her.

"—plus B squared . . ."

"Stop it! Let go of me!"

"—equals . . ."

"I said *stop*!"

"Hey, down there. What's the deal?" Something big banged on the bleachers above them. It had to be Coach Virile. Sophie would know that too-high-for-a-giant voice anywhere.

Ten

Come out of there!" Coach Virile said.

B.J. let go of Sophie's hand enough for her to pull away from Anne-Stuart's pen. Even as she rubbed her palm frantically on the side of her jeans, Sophie snatched up her backpack and wriggled out from under the bleachers.

Coach Virile looked at her. Then he banged on the bench again. "Come on out—let's go, ladies."

"Coming, Coach Nanini!" Julia purred.

Three Corn Pop bodies slithered out, and three kitty-cat faces softened up at the big coach. All Sophie could do was look at her palm. It was a smeary mess of black ink, but the partial formula still wavered its way through her handprint in permanent ink.

"Who gave you permission to go under there?" said the coach.

"We didn't know we needed permission," Julia said. Her eyes widened as she looked at the other two, who blinked in innocence.

"So I'm telling you that you do need permission," Coach Virile said. "And I'm telling you that I'm not giving it to you, and neither is anybody else."

"We're sorry!" Julia said.

"Totally," B.J. said.

Anne-Stuart gave a sniff Sophie was sure was supposed to sound tearful.

Coach Virile hooded his eyebrow in Sophie's direction. "What about you, Little Bit?"

Sophie put her hand behind her back. "I was invited in," she said. "I didn't know it was against the rules either."

She knew if Maggie were there she would say, "It isn't in the handbook."

"We'll find a legal place to meet, Coach," Julia said. She tilted her head at him the same way she did at Tod.

The three Pops turned to go, but Coach put up a meaty hand. "We're not done here," he said. "What was going on under there? Sounded like somebody was under duress."

The Corn Pops looked at him blankly. It was obvious to Sophie that they didn't even know what *duress* meant. She did, because she had been the one under it.

"We were just doing our girl thing," Julia said, once again cocking her head.

"Which is why I'm glad I'm not a girl," Coach Virile said. "Go on—get out of here."

"By-ee!" Julia sang out. And then the three of them ran like they had a pack of dogs after them.

Sophie didn't move. She knew they were going to be around some corner waiting for her with their Sharpie.

"What's in your hand, Little Bit?"

Sophie squeezed her fist tighter behind her back.

"Nothing," she said. "They were writing something on it, and I didn't want them to." She tried to smile. "I got in enough trouble for that face on my head."

Coach Virile grunted. "You want it off?"

"Yes," Sophie said. "But it's in Sharpie."

"I've got some stuff. Come on."

Sophie didn't even hesitate, except to ask as she followed him, "Will you give me a late pass?"

"Yes," he said. "If you'll also let me give you a little advice."

He motioned for her to sit down on a bench outside the boys' locker room. Sophie sat downand waited until he came out with a bottle of something and a rag. Her heart was slamming against the inside of her chest.

He sat down next to her and dumped what looked like half the contents of the bottle into the rag and held out his hand for Sophie's. She turned her palm up, and he went after it. She was sure he didn't even look at what it said.

"I've been doing a little observing since I caught you in the boys' locker room," he said as he scrubbed. "I haven't put it all together yet, but I think you're up against something that thinks it's bigger than you."

Sophie didn't answer.

"Sometimes in life you have to face things on your own," he said, still scrubbing, "and sometimes you can't. You have to have help." He stopped rubbing, examined her palm, and went back at it. "Growing up is about learning the difference."

But what if there's nobody there TO help? Sophie thought. *What if your friends get scared?*

"When people try to force you to do things you don't want to do," he went on, "when they try to take away your power, that's some serious stuff."

He stopped again and surveyed Sophie's hand. "I can take away ink—but I can't take away trouble unless somebody trusts me."

Sophie could hear a question in there, but she couldn't answer it. She could only stare at her now-clean palm and cry.

"You want me to take you to Coach Yates?" Coach Virile said.

"No, sir."

"Some other teacher? Maybe a counselor?"

Sophie shook her head. What would be the point? Who would believe her?

"Talk to somebody, Little Bit," Coach Virile said. His voice was as soft as Mama's. "Because whatever you're trying to carry is just too big for you."

"I'm okay," Sophie whispered. "I just need a pass to class."

As she hurried away from him, he said something she couldn't quite hear. It sounded like "Bless your heart, Little Bit."

But she was sure she was wrong.

There was a note waiting for Sophie on her desk when she got to first period. It wasn't folded like one of Fiona's birds. "Meet us on the track third period," it said in Anne-Stuart's curlicues.

Why? Sophie thought. *So you can make a cheat sheet all the way up my arm?*

Aurora shook her head. I have forgotten something—something I need in order to help fair Willow. Something more powerful than me—that will return my power to me. Aurora closed her eyes and searched. There were only kind eyes looking back at her, beckoning, pulling her—

"All right, class," Mrs. Clayton said, "the moment you've all been waiting for." She shot her bullet gaze across the rows. "We are handing back your Honor Code papers."

"We want you to correct all the grammatical errors we've indicated," Ms. Hess said. Her dimples poked in. "And for some of you, that will take considerable time."

Wooden frog earrings danced from her lobes. *Perfect*, Sophie thought, *to go with her frog-rubbery mouth*. She automatically looked at Fiona to see if she was noticing too. But

Fiona was riveted to Mrs. Clayton, and so was Darbie, as if they were afraid to let their eyes go wandering into trouble.

"Get started," Ms. Hess said as she put the last paper in Gill's hand. "Grammar books are on the shelf if you need them."

Sophie raised her hand. "I didn't get mine back," she said.

Ms. Hess and Mrs. Clayton looked at each other.

"Did you turn one in, Sophie?" Mrs. Clayton said, voice gruff.

"Yes!" Sophie said.

"I checked it off when they first came in," Ms. Hess said. "But I don't remember grading it." She looked at Mrs. Clayton again. "Do you?"

"Okay, don't panic," Mrs. Clayton said. "We'll check through everything. It's here someplace."

Since they didn't tell her what to do while everybody else was busy correcting, Sophie drew a line under Anne-Stuart's note and picked up her pen.

Aurora dipped into the ink and began to write. "I will meet you on the jousting field," she wrote, "but I will not have my sword or my spear. I will bring only my word that I will have no conversation with Willow before the test is put before me—or after. The maidens have all abandoned me for fear of being brought before the Court and punished, and so . . ."

Aurora paused, ink forming a teardrop at the end of the pen. Could she tell all these lies? How could she NOT tell them? Was this not the only way to find out the vixens' evil plan and reveal it to poor Willow before the tournament and Dance?

"Forgive me," she whispered, though she didn't know to whom. And then she wrote, "Since they have abandoned me, I care nothing for what happens to them now. I am on my own, a solitary lady, alone on her crusade for Truth."

She rolled the letter up and would have tied it with a lock of her hair except—

Sophie pulled out one of her shoelaces and wrapped it around the spindled note. She could take one out of her PE sneakers later. As corrected papers were being turned in, Sophie passed her message over to Anne-Stuart. Then she really wanted to wash her hands.

Toward the end of the block's second hour when the class was taking turns reading, an eighth grader slipped in and handed something to Mrs. Clayton. She hurried over to Sophie's desk.

"Good news, Sophie," she said in a raspy whisper. "We must have left your paper in the teachers' workroom and someone found it. We'll get it graded and back to you Monday."

When the bell rang, Sophie headed for the door. She could see Fiona and Darbie on the other side, craning their necks to see if she was coming, but Julia blocked her way.

"Walk to PE with us, Sophie," she said.

"We don't want you to be alone, now that your friends have dumped you," Anne-Stuart said.

Their voices made Sophie think of the artificial sugar stuff Mama put in her coffee. Anne-Stuart steered Sophie out the door, her hand on the strap of Sophie's backpack. "You said you'd meet us on the track anyway," she said. "At least, I *think* that's what your note said."

"You're still weird," Julia said. They were well out of Hess-Clayton earshot now, and she dropped the Sweet'N Low voice.

Sophie wanted to jerk away from Anne-Stuart and run straight to her Corn Flakes, who were not far ahead of them, zigzagging puzzled looks back at her through the crowd.

But if I do, she thought, *the Pops will know I was lying about not hanging with them anymore.*

Sophie met Fiona's eyes just as the Flakes rounded the corner. *Just trust me*, she tried to say with her own.

But by the time she and the Pops made the turn, Fiona was sending her a clear message back: *This is heinous.*

Then Fiona picked up her pace, and Maggie, Darbie, and finally Willoughby hurried to keep up with her.

"They really are ditching you," Julia said into Sophie's ear. "Too bad."

"Whatever," Sophie said. The word stuck in her throat, right there with the hippopotamus.

When they got to the locker room, with Cassie and B.J. now on the scene, the Pops kept Sophie from even getting to her locker—much less her friends—until most of the girls had cleared out.

"You're going to be late," Sophie said to B.J., who was breathing Cheetos breath into her face. "You guys should go."

"Like we're going to leave you alone," Cassie said. Her voice was shrill, as if she were back to trying to impress Julia.

She probably IS, Sophie thought as she fumbled with her lock. *Now that she almost told me one of their secrets, she's probably back to Step Two.*

When she turned around, T-shirt in hand, they were all standing there, staring. Something in Sophie began to shrivel like a raisin. They were going to watch her expose her very-flat chest and marvel at her little-girl-ness in the presence of all their bras and lip gloss and highlighted hair.

"What's the deal?" said a voice from the end of the row of lockers.

Sophie cringed. It was Coach Yates.

Why did she pick this day to come in here? she thought. *Is EVERYBODY watching me now?*

"Julia, B.J., Cassie, Anne-Stuart—you all look ready to me. Let's hit the door."

"We were waiting for Sophie," Julia said, pouring the Sweet'N Low in, three pink packets at a time.

"People who wait for Sophie get tardies and detentions," Coach Yates said. Her voice went up several yell-notches. "Cheerleaders who get tardies and detentions don't cheer at assemblies."

They all ran as if they'd been shot at. Sophie turned her back to Coach Yates and put her T-shirt between her teeth.

"LaCroix," Coach said.

Sophie opened her mouth to answer and dropped her shirt on the floor.

"I haven't figured you out, but I'm working on it. Anything you want to tell me?"

Sophie shook her head.

"Okay," Coach said. "Meet me outside. I have a job for you."

Sophie would rather have been shot herself. But she got into her PE clothes and joined Coach Yates at the edge of the track.

All during class, Coach had Sophie stand beside her and write down the girls' times as they took their running tests. At the end of class, after Sophie had copied all the entries over onto another sheet in pen, everybody was already leaving the locker room. At least the Corn Pops hadn't been able to harass her, but Miss Imes was sure going to if she was late.

"I have a test next period!" Sophie said. There wasn't even time to put in a new shoelace.

"I'll tell Miss Imes you're coming," Coach Yates said.

And she'll probably think I'm in trouble in PE again, Sophie thought as she hurried down the hall with one shoe gaping and flopping at the heel. The only good thing about it was that the Pops were already in their seats in the math room when she arrived, and Miss Imes didn't even let her sit down before she gave her the test and put her out in the hall.

At first Sophie was sure she had forgotten the formula by now, and she stared at the problems until her eyes blurred with tears.

"We've forgotten something," Aurora whispered.

Ya think? Sophie wanted to shout at her. *The Pops won't need the formula on my hand to convince Miss Imes I cheated, because I'm gonna fail—*

"A squared," she could almost hear Julia saying. *"Plus—"*

"That's it!" Sophie said out loud.

She wrote the formula at the top of her paper and went to work on the problems. Some of them were the exact ones in the book that she and Tod had worked on last night. Some needed that trick Lacie had taught her. But they all worked out. She was shaking when she handed the paper to Miss Imes.

"Did Fiona help you study?" Miss Imes said as her red pencil flicked down the page.

"No," Sophie said. "Tod did."

Miss Imes smiled faintly. "That's what I wanted to hear." She wrote a large number at the top of Sophie's paper and turned it toward her. "There you are," she said. "Ninety-five. I knew you could do it if you got serious."

Sophie was sure she was going to dissolve into a puddle before she could get to her desk. On the way she tried to catch Fiona's glance, but Fiona seemed to have eyes only for the assignment she and Darbie were working on together.

As she sat down, Miss Imes stood up and said, "Tod, I want to see you out in the hall."

"Busted!" Colton crowed.

Miss Imes gave him a look that could have frozen the sun.

When the bell finally rang for lunch, Sophie was the first one to the door, even from the back of the room. She had to get to Willoughby, and she had to do it in secret so the Corn Pops wouldn't see. Their threat to tell Miss Imes she'd cheated still hung over Sophie's head like an executioner's ax.

Aurora shook that off with a toss of her head that was so hard her pointed hat took off on the wind, its long veil trailing like a sail—

Tod flew past her sideways, grabbing for the beanie and clutching it against him like a football as he hit the ground.

"Score!" cried Eddie Wornom, thrusting his arms above his head.

"Over here!"

Sophie whirled around to see Colton catch the hat-pass Tod threw him. He jumped straight up with it, took a shot at an imaginary basket, and dunked Sophie's wadded-up beanie over the railing and down into the front lawn below.

"I guess you better go get that, Soapy," Julia said.

"You have to get permission to go out the front door first," Anne-Stuart said.

Cassie snorted. "Good luck finding somebody to let you out at lunchtime."

Sophie considered jumping over the side, but instead headed toward the stairs.

"To-od," Julia said. "Remember— "

"*What?*" he said.

Sophie left what sounded like true love going down the toilet behind her and navigated her way through everything the

Pops had predicted. Kids passed along the way, whispering things like "Why does that girl have her head shaved?" and "Is she the one who has leukemia?" and "She should wear a hat." By the time Sophie got through all that, it was too late to go to her locker and get her lunch. She wasn't hungry anyway.

Sophie wandered back upstairs to be close to the math room when the bell rang. Maybe she'd be able to catch Willoughby heading to class and pull her away to talk someplace where the Pops couldn't see her. As she headed toward it, Sophie trailed her hand along the railing—

Below Aurora, the sounds of the music for the ritual Dance lifted like colored scarves from the instruments. "She is going to look so LAME!" came a vixen cry.

Sophie pulled herself down into a crouch and peered down between the bars in the railing. Julia, B.J., and Anne-Stuart were just below her in the otherwise-empty courtyard with the three cheerleaders Sophie still didn't know. All eyes were on Julia.

"Okay, once more from the beginning," she said. She bobbed her ponytail at Cassie, who was sitting on the ground next to a boom box. Cassie pushed a button, and unfamiliar music pounded as the Pops formed a line and started their routine.

"Willoughby can't even do the moves," Cassie had told Sophie.

"And I guess they aren't going to help her learn them either," she whispered to herself.

But that still didn't make sense. Willoughby had been the best one at the tryouts. She practiced the routine everywhere but in the middle of Miss Imes's classroom.

As she continued to watch, Sophie could feel her eyes bulging. She'd never seen Willoughby practice *this* routine. This wasn't the one they were working on just yesterday.

The cheer ended with B.J. and Julia each putting a hand back to assist Anne-Stuart up to their shoulders, where she stood, arms raised in a *V*.

"This is where you'll come in later, Cass," Julia said.

"Yeah," B.J., said, "but for now, they'll laugh at *her* the way everybody laughed at *us* at tryouts!"

"Tell the world, B.J.," Julia said, glaring at her.

Anne-Stuart jumped down and went into a split, which opened up a space between Julia and B.J. Sophie didn't wait to see how Cassie fit into it. She crawled like a crab away from the railing and was running before she could even stand up straight. The shoe without the shoelace came off, but she kept going.

"Hey!" somebody shouted at her.

Sophie ran on, shoe squealing and sock sliding.

"I WAS watching her!" Tod yelled to somebody else.

His voice faded as Sophie took the stairs down two at a time and careened across the hall to the cafeteria door. Kids were lined up inside, ready to go to their classes when the bell rang, but Sophie was prepared to plow through all of them to get to Willoughby and tell her: *They're going to do a different cheer! They're going to make you look lame!*

Sophie skidded, arms flailing. A spattering of middle school laughter sprayed into the hall. She knew she looked like a crazy person, but she was so close—

Until somebody grabbed her and spun her around to face a Corn Pop wall.

Eleven

"You little rat!" Julia shouted at her.

"We saw you spying on us!"

"You were on your way to tell her, weren't you?"

"Tell who?" Sophie said.

It was all she could think of to say, because right now if she didn't get to Willoughby, she knew the Pops would probably change their plan, maybe to something worse, and Sophie would never know how to protect Willoughby from them. She had to convince them she wasn't going near Willoughby.

"Who do you think?" B.J. said.

Sophie adjusted her glasses with a casual hand and tried not to breathe too hard. "If you're talking about Willoughby, I told you: she's not my friend anymore. None of them are."

"You're just saying that," Anne-Stuart said. "She's just saying that, Julia."

"Then why were you watching us?" Julia said. Her green eyes narrowed.

"You mean why was I looking down on the courtyard?" Sophie said. "I was pretending I was Aurora—medieval maiden—and I was in one of the castle towers."

Julia turned to Anne-Stuart and rolled her eyes. B.J. abruptly poked her in the side, and in spite of Julia's glare, whispered in her ear. Julia slowly smiled.

"So you're just weird on your own now, Soapy?" Julia said. "You really don't 'play' with your strange little friends anymore?"

She looked almost convinced. Sophie squeezed her eyes shut for a second. *Forgive me*, she thought. And then she said, "They're just a bunch of flakes. I can't wait to see Willoughby make a moron out of herself, okay? So get off me!"

Julia shrugged her shoulders and said, "Okay. We believe you."

The bell rang and the Corn Pop wall broke and disappeared. But not before Julia looked over Sophie's head and laughed, right at someone.

Sophie didn't want to turn around. She already knew who that someone was. Who they all were.

But she did turn, and she saw her beloved Flakes looking at her. The hurt in their eyes cut Sophie to her Corn Flake core.

"I didn't mean what I said!" Sophie cried. "I found something out. And I have to make them think— "

But it was as if she weren't even talking. Darbie turned white and fled with Willoughby at her heels.

"That was totally against the Code, Sophie," Maggie said.

Fiona made a hard sound, something that wasn't a laugh or a sob or anything Sophie had ever heard come out of her best friend before.

"What Code?" Fiona said. "Sophie made it up, so I guess she can un-make it anytime she wants to."

Sophie could only beg them with her eyes because she couldn't speak. Not with Fiona looking as if Sophie had run her through with a sword.

All Sophie could hear in her brain for the rest of the day was, *I denied them.*

It didn't help to tell herself that everything she'd said and done had been for the good of her maidens. In fact, by sixth period, when Aurora tried to speak, Sophie shoved her into the back of her imagination and slammed the dungeon door on her.

I have to make them believe ME, not Aurora, Sophie told herself. She wrote Fiona a note during sixth period and came close to dropping it into Fiona's open backpack while nobody seemed to be looking, but Eddie dived for it and Sophie had to retrieve it.

On Saturday an ache spread through Sophie like a disease. Nobody answered her emails. Nobody would talk to her on the phone, and she didn't have the heart to call Kitty. She stayed in her room, sure that Mama and Daddy thought she was pouting about not having her camera. That was fine. She didn't want them or anybody else to know how badly she'd botched everything up.

I was only trying to protect Willoughby, she told herself. *I had to do what I had to do.*

That was when she did cry, long and hard. Because she'd never meant for what she had to do to take her so far from the Code, and from the Corn Flakes.

"I'm sorry," she sobbed into her pillow. "I'm sorry."

She was nearly cried out before she realized that, for the first time in what seemed like a very long while, she was talking to Jesus.

With her tear-swollen eyes it was hard to see him, but somewhere in the dark hurt, he was there. His eyes were kind. They hadn't changed at all.

Don't look at me that way! she cried out in her heart. *I don't deserve it! I broke the whole Code you gave us! I put people down—I let them take my power—and I turned INTO them!*

Still his eyes were kind.

"Just make it so it isn't true—make it so it didn't happen—please!"

"Oh, Dream Girl, I don't think anybody can do that."

Sophie froze, and for a moment she thought it was Jesus' touch she felt.

But it was Mama, gently stroking her back. "What is it that needs undoing?" she said.

"You'll think I'm hateful!" Sophie cried.

"Sounds like you're doing a pretty good job of that yourself. Come on, let's get it out where you can look at it, huh?"

For a few minutes, Mama's words, as kind as Jesus' eyes, made Sophie cry harder. Finally she sat up, sniffling like Anne-Stuart. She blew her nose and told Mama absolutely everything, from the beginning. It wasn't until she was finished that she realized the hippo was gone. But the ache was still there.

Mama put her elfin hands on the sides of Sophie's face and looked straight into her eyes. "Sophie Rae LaCroix," she said, "I want you to promise me something."

"I'm not very good at keeping promises anymore," Sophie said.

"Keep this one. Tell me that you will never, ever again try to handle something like this by yourself." She brushed a tear from Sophie's cheek. "Sometimes we have to handle things on our own—but this was not one of those times. The Corn Pops are getting more subtle with their bullying now that they're older, and that's harder to prove. But honey, it's going deeper, and it has to stop—or you girls *are* going to become like them."

Sophie studied Mama's face, all pulled in with concern, but she could hear Coach Virile's voice, saying the same things. Coach Virile's unibrow and Mama's soft forehead holding the same thoughts? It almost made Sophie smile.

"You can come to Daddy and me. You can talk to Dr. Peter—"

The tears were there again, choking at Sophie's throat. "I can't talk to Dr. Peter now," she said. "I didn't even do the assignment he gave us. I missed his class because of detention."

"You don't have to be perfect before you can come to any of us. If you waited for that, you'd never talk to us at all! We just count on you being honest."

Sophie felt everything on her sagging as she sank against the pillows. Mama ran a hand over her head. "Does all this mean you haven't been talking to Jesus either?" she said.

Sophie could hardly look at her. "Yes. How could I do that?"

"Just the way I do and Daddy does and even Dr. Peter does—sometimes for a few minutes, sometimes for weeks, even months. It's not that we don't know he's still there. We just forget we need to go to him."

"I bet you never lost all your friends and turned into a lying Corn Pop!"

"I don't think you did either," Mama said. "But you do have some things to take care of, and Daddy and I do too."

"I don't get it," Sophie said.

"Then let's go find Daddy. We'll all sit down and see what we can figure out."

They had a meeting, the three of them, down in the kitchen over Mama's double-chocolate brownies, which Mama ate four of.

"I'm glad you're better," Sophie said to her.

Mama smiled at Daddy as she chewed. "We're going to have a LaCroix team meeting about that soon," he said. "But let's get this cleared up first."

After she and Mama and Daddy talked and came up with a plan, it looked like there might be hope. It didn't keep Sophie from sobbing while she was trying to imagine Jesus that night, but it did make it easier to face Dr. Peter the next morning.

When he greeted her with his twinkly eyes and a burst of "Sophie-Lophie-Loodle! I've missed you!" Sophie burst into tears again.

"Your mom told me what happened," he said as he located a box of Kleenex. "She said you're feeling pretty lousy."

"I think I flunked that test you were talking about," Sophie said. "I'm even having trouble looking at Jesus."

"Been there," Dr. Peter said. He opened his Bible on his lap. "So was that other Peter. Simon Peter." His voice got Dr. Peter soft and he tapped the Bible. "You ready to go back in?"

Sophie nodded and closed her eyes.

"Okay. Imagine that you are Simon and you're with Jesus when a bunch of soldiers and big muckety-mucks come to take him away."

"Do we have to read about Simon denying Jesus three times?" Sophie said. "I feel bad enough already. I know I did that too."

"Knowing it is a good start," Dr. Peter said. "The next step is to ask Jesus to forgive you."

"Will he?" Sophie said.

"When you're truly sorry—always."

"I am!" Sophie said. "I am SO sorry!"

"Tell him," Dr. Peter said.

Sophie closed her eyes, but before she could even wrap the words around her sorriness, she could see the forgiveness in those kind eyes. When she opened her own eyes, Dr. Peter was watching her.

"The next step is to ask him to help you hear him next time," he said.

Sophie nodded sadly. "BEFORE I mess up."

"Okay—come on," Dr. Peter said. "Let's skip to the good part." He fanned the pages of the Bible until he landed on a spot. "Simon's hanging out by a fire near where they've taken Jesus. He's already denied knowing Jesus twice. People keep harassing him about it, and finally somebody says he *knows*

Simon was with Jesus by their similar accents. Now, Luke twenty-two, verse sixty. Imagine—"

Sophie closed her eyes again, *and Sophie/Simon poked his freezing hands toward the fire and wished these people would just leave him alone. Everything was so confusing right now. He didn't need all these questions—*

Dr. Peter read: "'Peter replied, "Man, I don't know what you're talking about!" Just as he was speaking, the rooster crowed. The Lord turned and looked straight at Peter. Then Peter remembered the word the Lord had spoken to him: "Before the rooster crows today, you will disown me three times." And he went outside and wept bitterly.'"

Sophie didn't have to imagine that part. She was already doing it.

"I know how he feels!" she wailed. "I shouldn't have lied, no matter what!"

Dr. Peter handed Sophie another Kleenex. "Let me ask you something, Loodle," he said. "Where were all the other disciples when Simon Peter was sitting right there where people could ask him questions?"

"I don't know," Sophie said. "Hiding?"

"Yeah, they pretty much split. And why do you think he hung around?"

Sophie didn't have an answer for that one.

"Okay," Dr. Peter said. He rubbed his hands together. "Why did you hang out with Cassie when you had detention and 'spy' on the Pops when they were practicing their fool-Willoughby cheerleading routine?"

"Because I was trying to find out what they were going to do to Willoughby."

Dr. Peter was quiet. Sophie blinked at him. "Is that what Simon Peter was doing?"

"Could be. The point is, he didn't abandon Jesus completely, just like you didn't abandon Willoughby or the Code."

"But Peter ended up lying when people asked him, and so did I!"

"Don't you hate it when you're human?" Dr. Peter said. "Why did you tell the Pops that the Flakes weren't your friends anymore?"

"Because I wanted them to think I wouldn't tell Willoughby what I found out. But then all my friends believed it too!"

"That's the trouble with lying, even when we think we're doing it for the right reason. When did you feel the absolute worst about it?"

Sophie didn't even hesitate. "When I turned around and I knew they heard what I said about them and they all had this hurt look in their eyes."

Dr. Peter looked back at the Bible. " 'The Lord turned and looked straight at Peter. Then Peter remembered.' "

"But it was too late then," Sophie said.

Dr. Peter put the Bible on the floor and leaned back in his chair. "The thing is, Loodle, Simon Peter couldn't have saved Jesus no matter what he did. That wasn't his job."

"What was it then?"

"When Jesus came back after his resurrection— "

"Did he get all up in Simon Peter's face?" she said.

"Is that what you're afraid of?" Dr. Peter said.

"Yes."

"Let's see about that." He turned to the Bible. " 'Jesus said to Simon Peter, "Do you truly love me more than these?" "Yes, Lord," he said, "you know that I love you." Jesus said, "Feed my lambs." ' "

Sophie/Simon saw Jesus' kind eyes and heard the words she wasn't expecting.

"'Again Jesus said, "Simon son of John, do you truly love me?" He answered, "Yes, Lord, you know that I love you." Jesus said, "Take care of my sheep." The third time he said to him—'"

"Don't you believe me, Jesus?" Sophie burst out. "This is the third time you've asked me that!" She bit at her lip. "I'm sorry, Dr. Peter—go ahead."

"How many times did he deny Jesus, Loodle?"

"Three," Sophie said.

Dr. Peter was quiet, until Sophie slowly nodded her head.

"Just like you, Sophie, Simon Peter was hurt because Jesus kept asking him. He said, 'Lord, you know all things; you know that I love you.'"

He stopped reading. Sophie's eyes blinked open.

"So what did Jesus say?" Sophie said.

Dr. Peter's eyes looked a little wet to her. "He said, 'Feed my sheep.' He gave Simon Peter three chances to show his love, one for every time he had been too afraid to before. And now he was showing him he trusted him again. He gave him a job to do: taking care of all the people who needed to find Jesus."

"Did Peter do it?" Sophie said.

"Until the day he died," Dr. Peter said. "I'm proud to be named after him."

Sophie closed her eyes. She didn't see herself as Simon Peter anymore. And she didn't see Aurora. She just saw herself—shrimpy, flat-chested, almost-bald-headed Sophie—ready to do what she and Mama and Daddy had decided she should do.

"I think you get it, Loodle," Dr. Peter said.

She gave him a wispy smile. "I think I do too," she said.

Twelve

The next morning Daddy dropped her off in front of GMMS with the assurance that he and Mama would probably see her there before the day was over. Sophie breathed in a prayer and went straight to Ms. Hess' room. Sophie was sure Ms. Hess' creamy dimples flattened when she saw her. Even the silver angels dangling from her earlobes didn't look all that happy.

Sophie said, "Ms. Hess, I need to talk to you about something serious." Her voice cracked on its way up, and Sophie was sure that was the only reason Ms. Hess put down her chalk and pointed to a chair.

Sophie told her she was sorry she had messed up the cheerleading tryouts and said sarcastic things in class, and then she explained to her what she knew about the cheerleaders' plan. The angels stopped swinging against Miss Hess' cheeks. "You're making a pretty serious accusation, Sophie," she said. "Did anyone else see this go down except Cassie?"

"Tod Ravelli," Sophie said. "But I think he was supposed to be keeping me away from Willoughby so I couldn't tell her, and I guess he lost me."

Miss Hess pressed her fingers against her forehead and closed her eyes. Sophie's heart sagged. She knew what was coming next.

"I have to tell you, Sophie," Ms. Hess said, "I have my reasons not to trust you. The people you're talking about aren't perfect. But I don't see *them* clowning around in class and getting detention and trying to make fools of people." She pressed her rubbery lips together before she added, "Give me one reason why I should believe you."

"I think I have one right here." Mrs. Clayton crossed over to them from the doorway of their office, holding a paper, which she handed to Ms. Hess. Her bullet eyes were on Sophie, but they weren't shooting at her.

"Your Code of Honor paper," she said. "Is everything in here true?"

"Yes, ma'am," Sophie said.

"We didn't get a better essay than this one, Ms. Hess," Mrs. Clayton said. "And I believe in its sincerity. I think it might be time for that Round Table we've been talking about."

Ms. Hess looked up from Sophie's paper and stared at her. "I think maybe you're right," she said.

The first bell rang, and they told Sophie not to say anything to anyone else about the cheerleading thing for now. Sophie sat at her desk and pretended to get a head start on the assignment on the board while she prayed and prayed and prayed. Ms. Hess took Julia and Anne-Stuart—looking all important in their cheerleading uniforms—out of the room.

They were gone for about twenty minutes. When they returned, Julia's eyes, glittering with menace, went straight to Sophie. Then Ms. Hess called Sophie into the hall. There wasn't a dimple within a hundred miles.

"I had them do their cheer for today's assembly," she said. "They did the one I've seen them practicing."

Sophie wasn't surprised.

"But there was one little glitch that made me think." Ms. Hess stopped and fiddled with one of the angels. "I told them that had better be the cheer I see at this afternoon's assembly. Between now and then, they know that if anyone wants to speak with me privately, I'll be available."

Aurora would go after them and slash something around and make them tell! Sophie thought. She sucked in air. *But I just have to be Sophie and be honest and get help. That's where the power is.*

Sophie felt the hippo in her throat shrink a little. There would be no making a fool of Willoughby at the assembly. At least not the way the Pops had planned.

But as Sophie made her way through the rest of first and second periods, she knew that was only a temporary fix. What was to keep the Pops from going at her again—or at any of them—now that they were so mad their lip gloss was frying?

It was hard to keep back the tears when her Flakes all gathered around Willoughby in the locker room third period, even when Coach Yates came in again and stood at the end of the row of lockers. At least the Pops were too busy saying, "How you doing, Coach?" in their sugar-substitute voices to get to Sophie.

Sophie was all the way changed into her PE clothes before she realized she hadn't bothered to cover herself up to hide her chest. Straightening her shoulders, she tossed her bandanna back into her locker and headed outside, bare-headed. *Be honest and get help*, she kept saying to herself. *You're still there, right, Jesus?*

Out on the field Sophie stood on tiptoe and searched through the milling girls for Willoughby. But Willoughby wasn't with the other Corn Flakes. With her heart in her throat Sophie looked harder, visions of the Pops with Willoughby in some corner flashing through her mind. But none of the Pops were around either, until Coach blew her whistle and they suddenly appeared, cheeks flushed. There was still no Willoughby.

The minute Coach turned them loose to do their warm-up laps, Sophie ran straight for Fiona. It didn't matter how the Flakes treated her. It was all about Willoughby right now. When she reached them, they were gazing out in three different directions, hands shading their eyes.

"Are you looking for Willoughby?" Sophie said.

"Yes," Fiona said. "Where is she?"

"I don't know! Last time I saw her she was talking to you guys."

"She started to tell us something about the cheerleaders," Maggie said.

"Don't tell Sophie anything," Fiona said. Her voice was cold. "She's not our friend, remember?"

"Fiona, don't make a bags of it," Darbie said. She was peering intently at Sophie. "Something's wrong, isn't it, Sophie?"

Sophie told them about the fool-Willoughby cheer, and how Ms. Hess had told the cheerleaders they better do the real one at the assembly.

"That must be what she was trying to say before she disappeared," Maggie said. Her flat, practical voice was like a slap somebody needed. Fiona looked all around Sophie but not quite at her.

"I don't like the way this is sounding," Darbie said. "I think we should find her and make sure she's all right."

Fiona turned, but Sophie grabbed her arm. "I know how to do this now—not like we *were* doing it. You have to believe me."

"Why should we?" Fiona said. For a flicker of a moment her eyes had that same hurt look that had haunted Sophie all weekend.

"Fiona, can you ever lay off?" Darbie said. "Tell us what you're thinking, Sophie."

"First, we ask the Pops if they've seen Willoughby," Sophie said. "Just ask them. Don't be funny or mean or anything—"

Fiona didn't say anything.

"I'll take Julia," Sophie said. "Will you guys ask the rest of them?"

Coach Yates blew the whistle, and they scattered down the track. Julia, with her long stride, was hard to keep up with.

"Where's Willoughby?" Sophie said.

Julia didn't even look down at her. "It's not my day to watch her."

Sophie slowed down and waited for Darbie to come around to her. She and Maggie had gotten the same answers from Anne-Stuart and B.J.

"We need to ask Cassie," Sophie said.

"Fiona couldn't find her," Darbie said.

Sophie felt a little ping inside. "Fiona wanted to help?"

Darbie smiled at her. "It'll be all right, Sophie," she said. "Fiona's just stubborn, that one."

Sophie ran toward Coach Yates. The prayer in her head was hardly words now, but it was there.

"Do you know where Willoughby is, Coach?" Sophie said.

Coach Yates ran her eyes down the list on her clipboard. "She never checked in." She frowned. "I thought I saw her in the locker room though."

"She *was* in the locker room," said Maggie, suddenly at Sophie's side with Darbie and Fiona.

"You think she's cutting class?" Coach Yates said.

"No!" they all said together. It was a glorious chorus of Corn Flakes.

"If she is, she won't cheer in the assembly this afternoon," Coach Yates said.

"And that's exactly why she wouldn't cut!" Sophie said.

"All right." To Sophie's surprise, Coach Yates gave Sophie's shoulder a pat. "You girls go on and do your laps, and I'll look for her."

It was hard not to continue their search, and Darbie, Fiona, Maggie, and Sophie all swept the horizon with their eyes as they ran. Together. No one seemed to know what to say, but Sophie was afraid she wouldn't get another chance like this.

"I'm sorry I lied about you being my friends," she said. "I was trying to get information out of the Pops—and I just ended up acting like them."

"No doubt," Fiona said.

"Fiona!" Darbie barked at her.

"Well, I thought we were supposed to be honest and live by the Code."

"We didn't live by the Code when we didn't defend Sophie to Miss Imes," Maggie said.

"You've already said that like ninety times, Maggie," Fiona said.

"Maybe she should say it ninety more until you stop being so wretchedly stubborn," Darbie said. "I, for one, forgive you, Sophie. I've been desperate for you. And so has Fiona."

Actually, Fiona didn't look that desperate to Sophie. She didn't look anything, except like she was still avoiding meeting Sophie's eyes.

"All I can say," Sophie told them, "is that I learned we have to be honest and get help when we need it. Especially from God. I, like, totally stopped thinking about Jesus, and that's when I got really messed up."

Her throat was getting hippo-thick again, and she was glad the bell rang. Fiona took off like a jet toward the locker room.

"I'll talk to her, Sophie," Darbie said. "Come on, Maggie."

Once again Sophie was left without her Corn Flakes, but at least there was a tiny, birthday-candle flame of hope. She tried not to drag her feet as she headed in, but she was still near the tail end of the crowd that was pushing its way into the two locker rooms. She was wedged between a bevy of shoving boys and the wall when she heard angry voices coming from behind her, in the alcove where the water fountain was. They weren't loud, but they were familiar, and they shot into Sophie's ears like arrows.

"I'm not doing any more of your dirty work, Julia," said Tod. He spat out her name like it was a bad word. "I'm not your slave."

"Come on, Tod."

"Is it the *N* or the *O* you don't get?" Tod said. "I'm not doing it."

The crowd was thinning, and Julia lowered her voice so that Sophie had to strain to hear. "Then how are we supposed to make it look like Willoughby was hooking up with a guy instead of going to class?"

"I guess you can't," Tod said. Sophie could hear his voice moving away.

"We have to!" Julia said.

"You're psycho," Tod said.

Sophie peeled herself off the wall and dodged around the last few girls to get to Coach Yates's office. But she wasn't in there, or in the locker room.

Coach Virile! Sophie thought as she ran back out into the hall. She considered bursting into the boys' locker room, but she decided not to go *there* again. She had to find him, because suddenly she knew right where Willoughby was, and who was keeping her there. *Get help*, her inside voice told her. *Don't try to do this alone.* But what was she supposed to do if the help wasn't around?

Praying with nothing but big gulps of air, Sophie shoved through the doors into the gym and ran toward the bleachers. She wiggled her way between the wall and the benches and stopped inside the Pops' secret hideaway with a squeal of sneakers.

Cassie was standing up with her back to Sophie, blocking her view, but Sophie darted around her and threw her arms around a sobbing Willoughby, who was crouched on the floor.

"Too late, LaCroix," Cassie said. She sounded so much like Julia it gave Sophie a creepy chill. "She's about to be suspended for being under here with a boy when she was supposed to be in class. Bye-bye, cheerleading."

Sophie pulled Willoughby tight against her. "I don't see a boy."

"I do."

Before Sophie could even register that it was Julia talking, not Cassie, Julia grabbed her arm and wrenched her away from Willoughby

Thirteen

When are you gonna get it, Little Boy LaCroix?" Julia said. "You can't stop us. You're not GIRL enough!"

Sophie tried to pull away, but Julia grabbed at Sophie's T-shirt and yanked so hard Sophie's arm came out of the sleeve.

"They will never believe you bunch of losers!" Julia said between her teeth.

She reached over Sophie's head and clawed at her back, and Sophie could feel her T-shirt rising up to her neck. Julia's other hand was grabbing at the sleeve that was still on.

"You are the whacked-out freak losers!" Julia said, and with a final snatch she hauled the shirt over Sophie's head, knocking her glasses off and sending them flying. "They will always believe us, because we are the winners!"

She dangled the T-shirt in front of Sophie's face and laughed from someplace deep and dark.

Above them, the bleachers started to rattle. Cassie screamed.

"I think you just lost that round, Julia," said the too-high-for-a-man's voice Sophie was coming to love. "So come out with your hands up."

Cassie bolted for the opening like a bunny on the run. Julia gave Sophie one last smug look and hurled her T-shirt into the dark abyss of the bleachers.

"Good luck explaining why you're half naked," she whispered. And then she strolled toward the opening, calling out, "You are not going to believe what I found under here, Coach Nanini!"

"Let's go — all of you!"

Julia slid out, and Sophie fumbled for her glasses, squinting to see Willoughby. But she wasn't there.

"Willoughby!" Sophie said. "Come on — all we have to do is be honest. You don't have to hide!"

"I'm not hiding," said a faint little voice. "I just had to get this."

Willoughby emerged from the shadows, holding Sophie's T-shirt.

"I think you need to put this on," she said. "'Cause you don't look *anything* like a boy."

Coach Virile was already chewing Julia and Cassie out by the time Sophie pulled on her now-grimy shirt, found her glasses, and got out with Willoughby.

"The first thing you better do," he was shouting at them, "is get rid of this idea that you can do anything you want to anybody you want. That stops right here!"

"I don't think that!" Julia said. "Do I, Cassie?"

"I heard every word you said down there," Coach Virile said. "You going to call *me* a liar now?"

"No," Julia said. She flipped her ponytail toward Sophie and Willoughby. "*They* are the liars. You don't know them, but they have been trying to get us in trouble ever since sixth grade."

Coach Virile was looking at Sophie and Willoughby. "What happened, Willoughby?"

Sophie slid her hand into Willoughby's. "Just tell the truth," she said. "I didn't before, and I messed everything up."

Julia rolled her eyes. Cassie didn't seem to have the strength to roll hers. Her face was the color of Cream of Wheat.

Willoughby squeezed Sophie's hand until she was sure her fingers were going to pop off. "Before class," she said in a voice Sophie could barely hear, "they told me Ms. Hess wanted to meet with the cheerleaders again in here, and then they said they would go check me in with Coach Yates. But then just Cassie came back, and she shoved me under the bleachers and told me all this horrible stuff about my friends. Especially Sophie. And she wouldn't let me out."

Julia crossed her arms, teacher-style. "Cassie, how could you do something like that?"

"Because you made me!" Cassie said.

"Liar!"

Coach Virile stuck out his arm just as Julia lunged forward. "Give it up, Julia," he said. "It's over."

He herded Julia and Cassie across the gym, calling over his shoulder, "Little Bit, you and Willoughby go on."

Willoughby clung to Sophie like a baby koala. "Is it really over, Sophie?" she said.

Sophie nodded. But when Julia looked back from the doorway with war in her eyes, Sophie wasn't sure it was ever going to be over.

Before Sophie could explain anything to the Flakes in the locker room, a note came for her to go to the office. The secretary there directed Sophie to a room marked *Conference.*

THIS can't be good, she thought.

But once she got inside, she couldn't quite think anything. Around a table sat Mrs. Clayton, Ms. Hess, Miss Imes, Coach Yates, Coach Virile, and Mr. Stires, all looking somehow different away from their usual domains. She was so startled she couldn't think of the name of the curly-haired man with the equally curly beard who sat with them, although she knew he was the principal. The only thing that kept her from bolting was the sight of Mama and Daddy smiling at her.

"Welcome to the Round Table, Sophie," Mrs. Clayton said. "Please join us."

Sophie went straight to Mama and squeezed into the chair with her. Across the table, Coach Virile grinned. That was reassuring. But still she blurted out, "Am I in trouble?"

"No, Sophie, you are not," Miss Imes said. "Coach Nanini, do you want to explain?"

Coach Virile's eyebrow went into a stern line. "Little Bit, I hope you've been bullied for the last time—you and every other student in this school. It's time we did something about this power thing that's going down, and we want you to help us."

"Me?" Sophie said.

"Who better?" Coach Yates said. She pulled her whistle lanyard back and forth. "You're the feistiest little kid I ever saw."

"What do you want me to do?" Sophie said.

"Mr. Bentley?" Mrs. Clayton said.

They all looked at Mr. Principal, whose beard and mustache parted for a smile. "I think your teachers are right when they say you should be one of the students at the core of our new program to show kids how to work out their differences and put a stop to bullying at GMMS."

"Oh," Sophie said. She could feel her voice going into squeak mode with nervousness. But then the words just came out from where she'd been living them all day.

"All I know to do is be honest," she said. "And get help when you need it." She shrugged. "You have to do that so you can take back your power to be yourself."

"What did I tell you?" Mrs. Clayton said. Even Ms. Hess showed her dimples.

"That's exactly what this new program is going to be based on," Mr. Bentley said. "We're going to train you and some other core students, and our goal is that pupils at GMMS will learn how to respect the dignity of every human being."

"Like a Code of Honor," Sophie said.

"Exactly."

"We've all watched your struggles in seventh grade," Miss Imes said. Heads around the table bobbed. "But your parents have come in and shared some things with us. I read your Honor Code paper in the teachers' room, and I hope you'll forgive me, but I showed it to Mr. Stires before I turned it in. That's why I agree with everyone else that you are turning into a fine young woman."

Daddy grinned like Sophie had just won the Super Bowl all by herself.

When the Round Table meeting was over, Miss Imes and Mrs. Clayton handed Mama and Daddy Sophie's latest papers—the 95 and the A+.

"Okay, Soph," Daddy said. "Looks like you've earned back that video camera."

Miss Imes stopped on her way to the door and nudged Mr. Stires. "Video camera?" she said.

"My friends and I make movies," Sophie said.

"From original scripts," Mama put in.

"We were making one about medieval maidens, but then I got busted."

"Be sure that there is no more 'busting,'" Miss Imes said, her mouth twitching. "Mr. Stires and I have been talking about starting a film club. It sounds like you need to be in it—you and those other little imps you hang around with."

"Family meeting tonight," Daddy said before he and Mama left.

"With GOOD news," Mama said.

The prospect of something that didn't involve Sophie on the hot seat sang through her. But as Sophie floated off to class, Aurora suddenly appeared—

She gave a deep, sweeping bow that dipped her sleeves to the ground. "It is time for me to release you, maiden," she said, "so that you can become Cecilia B. DeMovie, great twenty-first-century film director."

Sophie could already picture herself with a black beret covering her spiky hair, sitting in a canvas chair, shouting, "Cut!"

But Aurora whispered once more in her ear, "*Don't forget what we failed to remember in our mission together. What King Arthur discovered he had put aside, why the Round Table crumbled—*"

"I know," Sophie whispered back.

She stopped at the railing and closed her eyes. "I love you," she whispered to Jesus. "And I'll always remember."

Glossary

abyss [a-BISS] a hole or space so deep and scary that when you look into it you can't see the bottom

accustomed [a-KUS-tuhmed] when things are done in a way that you're used to

ammunition [am-yu-NI-shun] something embarrassing that can be fired back at you like bullets

assurance [a-SHUR-ance] a promise that puts your mind at ease

beckoning [BEH-kun-ing] a way of signaling someone to come closer without words

bevy [BEHV-ee] a large group

blaggards [BLAG-ghards] an Irish pronunciation of "black-guards," which are very rude and offensive people

brandishing [BRAN-dish-ing] waving something around in a threatening way

bronchial spasms [BRON-key-al SPA-zims] literally, when the tubes in your lungs go out of control from laughter, which could only mean something is incredibly funny

chivalry [SHI-val-ree] a code of honesty, kindness, and thinking of others before yourself; something usually associated with knights or thoughtful boyfriends

cowering [COW-er-ing] becoming very shy and wanting to run and hide when something scary comes

discouraged [dis-CUR-aged] how you feel when you lose confidence in yourself

duress [der-RES] extremely stressed to the point you just want to hide from the world

eejit [eeg-it] the way someone from Ireland might say "idiot"

enthusiastic [in-thew-zee-AST-ick] really excited and happy about something

executioner [eck-sa-KEW-shun-er] a person who is paid to put criminals to death

feistiest [FIE-stee-ist] very energetic and spirited compared to other people; a person who doesn't give up

gnaw [nawd] chewing on something over and over again

heinous [HEY-nus] unbelievably mean and cruel

icily [I-sill-ee] looking at someone in a very cruel way so it seems like icicles are shooting from your eyes

impediment [im-PE-di-ment] an obstacle that keeps something from happening, or at least slows it down

javelin [jahv-lin] a long pointy stick; it can be used for sport—to see how far it can be thrown into a field—or as a weapon

jousting tournament [JOWST-ing tur-na-ment] a type of entertainment in the Middle Ages when two armored knights would mount horses and charge at each other with long wooden poles, trying to knock each other off horseback

loathe [lowth] really, really hating something

maiden [MAY-den] a young unmarried woman

make a bags of [mayk a baygs of] do a poor job at, or screw things up

medieval [me-DEE-vul] something or someone from the Middle Ages, which lasted from the fifth century to the fifteenth century; this wasn't a fun time to live in, but it is now remembered for castles, knights, and fair maidens

ponder [POHN-der] to think really hard about something

puppeteer [puh-peh-TEER] someone who controls puppets on a stage

round table [ROWND taybull] according to stories about King Arthur, there was a special circular table where all the bravest knights in the kingdom met to discuss their good deeds

sarcastic [sar-CAS-tik] comments that are meant to hurt people

sheath [sheeth] a protective cover for a really sharp sword; it's sometimes carried on a person's hip

smugly [SMUG-lee] looking at someone in a proud "look what I did" way

slagging [slag-ging] mocking or making fun of someone

squabbling [SKWAH-bling] arguing wildly over something

surveillance [ser-VAY-lence] secretly watching someone in an attempt to gather proof they're doing something wrong

swaggering [SWAG-gur-ing] walking around in a way that is supposed to make people think you're important, but usually ends up making you look silly

vexed [veckst] completely confused and upset because of something that happened

villain [vil-an] a person who is basically evil, constantly trying to do bad things

virile [VEAR-il] the definition of manly; muscular, strong, and really hunky. Think cute movie star meets not-so-icky body builder

vixen [VICK-sin] a female villain; also means a woman or young girl who is mean

wench [whench] in medieval times, this was a servant girl, or the lowest class there was; it's also a mean insult

whacked-out [WHAKT-owt] crazy, out of your mind

wistfully [WHIST-ful-ee] longingly, wishing you could be part of something again